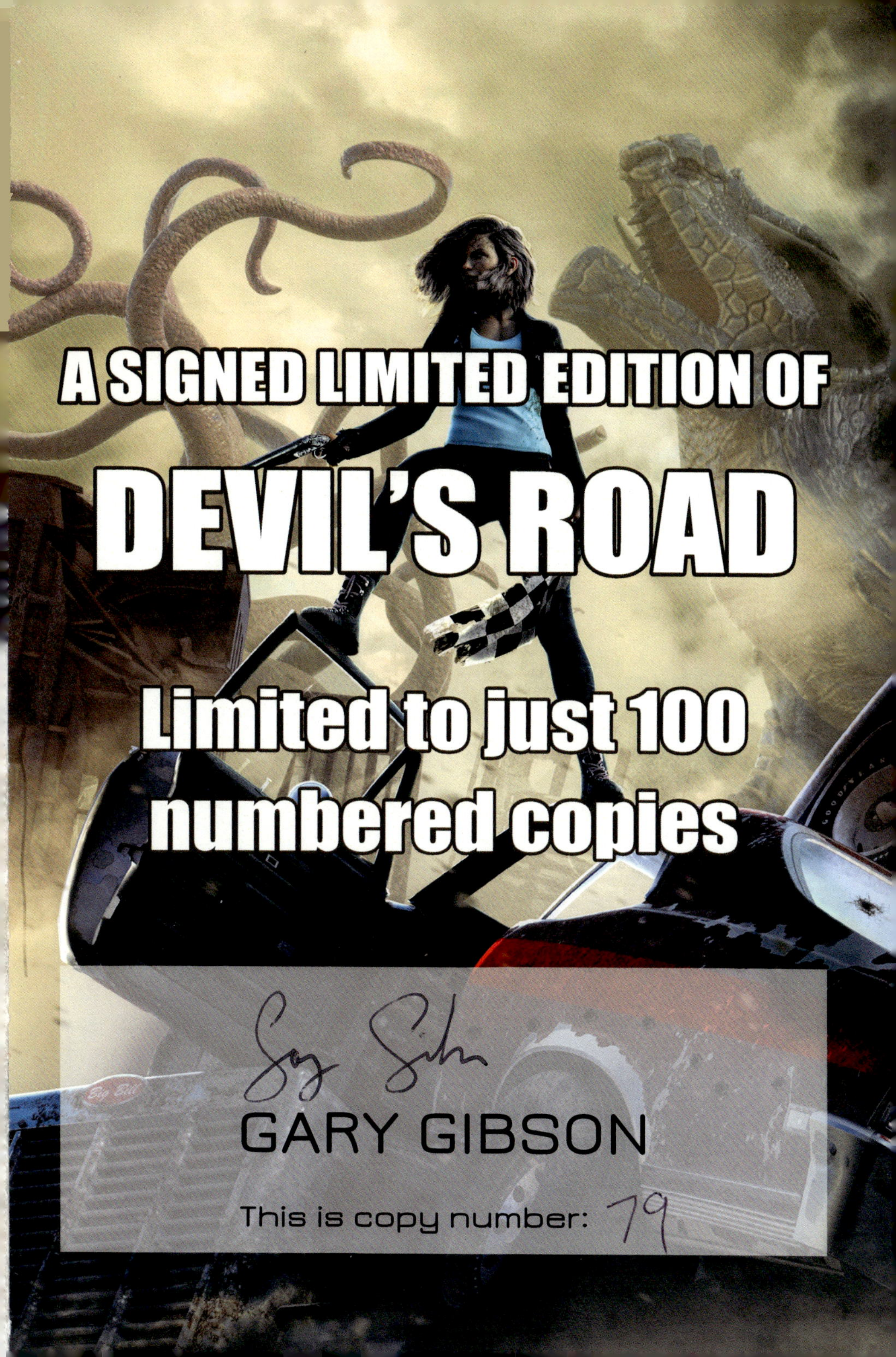
A SIGNED LIMITED EDITION OF
DEVIL'S ROAD
Limited to just 100 numbered copies
GARY GIBSON
This is copy number: 79

# DEVIL'S ROAD

# DEVIL'S ROAD

## A TALE OF GUNS, CARS AND KAIJU

Gary Gibson

NEWCON PRESS

NewCon Press
England

First published in the UK, March 2020 by
NewCon Press
41 Wheatsheaf Road,
Alconbury Weston,
Cambs, PE28 4LF

NCP222 (limited edition hardback)

10 9 8 7 6 5 4 3 2 1



ISBN:

978-1-912950-47-8 (hardback)

Cover art by J Caleb Design
Cover layout by Ian Whates and J Caleb Design

Typesetting and minor editorial meddling by Ian Whates
Book layout by Storm Constantine

# JAIL BREAK

Before the riot started and the cannibal came looking for her, Dutch McGuire dreamt she sat behind the wheel of a '69 Ford Mustang that rode low on the road, its chassis stiffened from high torque, the starred and broken tarmac of a desert highway reduced to a smooth blur beneath its wheels. A city rose up at the end of the road, and a great beast prowled through its streets, sweeping apartment buildings into dust as it searched for her. She should have been afraid, yet she felt nothing but a kind of serenity emanating from somewhere deep in her bones.

At last the beast faded away, and the city, and Dutch woke to unexpected darkness.

She blinked and sat up. For as long as Dutch had been an inmate the cell-block lights burned twenty-four seven from behind metal grilles, but for the first time they were dark. Indeed, the very absence of light had been sufficient to wake her.

She listened, hearing others come awake and calling to each other. A series of mechanical clicks and thuds echoed up and down the steel-grey corridor outside her cell, as if every door in the block had come unlocked at once.

For a moment the whole of the cell-block fell deathly quiet, followed by an uproar of yelling.

Yara stirred and muttered something foul in Russian from the bunk above Dutch's, her voice still thick with sleep.

Dutch swung her feet onto the cold concrete floor and listened to the shouts of the other inmates. Judging by what she could hear, nobody else had any idea what had happened. She stood and touched the barred door of their cell. It slid open with ease.

Well, she thought. That's what you got for relying on a centralised computer-controlled prison system.

Dutch stared at the corridor beyond until a sudden thought sent her to the cell's one tiny window, which looked out across the prison yard. She had to stand on tiptoe, but from what she could see, the cell block on the far side of the yard had also gone dark – and if both blocks were thus affected, she might as well assume the whole damn prison had gone dark.

Dutch listened. It sounded as if some of the shouting came from there too.

She grabbed hold of the iron bars in front of the glass and pulled herself up so she could get a better view. She looked across the yard in time to see a door come crashing open. Inmates spilled out in a flood, some carrying improvised weapons.

Dutch dropped back down and searched under her mattress until she found the bar of soap hidden there. She fumbled with it, cursing when the bar slipped out of her hands, picking it up once more and breaking it apart to reveal a shank.

Yara swung her legs over the side of her bunk and looked down at her. 'What the fuck is going on?' she asked in Russian.

'Riot,' said Dutch. 'Or some kind of mass breakout. Maybe both.' By now, her sight had adjusted to the darkness.

Yara levered her immense bulk out of her bunk, climbing down beside Dutch and flexing arms made thick and ropy with muscle from long hours of weight-lifting. 'A riot?' she asked with ill-concealed enthusiasm. 'What started it?'

'I don't know. But all the cell doors just came unlocked at once.'

Yara let out a heavy breath, her broad, meaty hands flexing at her sides. Once, Yara told Dutch she'd considered a career as a Sumo wrestler before killing three men in a brawl. 'All of them?' she asked.

Dutch nodded. 'Far as I can tell, yeah. The other blocks look like they're all opened up too.'

'The guards?'

'Are vastly outnumbered,' said Dutch. 'We don't have much time.'

Yara's heavy brows drew together. 'You're making a run for it?'

'Aren't you?'

Yara's lips pressed together in a thin line of disapproval. 'Why even try? They can find us easily enough.'

She meant the tracker chip embedded deep beneath the skin of every prisoner, of course. 'Yara,' asked Dutch, 'exactly when is your release date?'

You could almost picture the wheels clicking into place one after the other whenever Yara thought through anything of sufficient complexity. 'I don't have a release date,' she said at last, glancing at the open cell door.

'Me neither,' said Dutch. 'So since they're never going to let either of us out, what else is there to do but run while we have the chance?'

'But –'

Dutch touched the other woman's wrist. 'There are more

than a thousand prisoners, Yara. They can't catch every last one of us.'

Yara nodded with a ponderous motion and reached out with her other hand. Dutch hesitated before grasping both of Yara's hands in hers, wincing at the other woman's powerful grip.

'Good luck,' said Yara. 'And watch out for Anna. She still hates your guts.'

'I'll be gone before Anna can find me,' said Dutch. 'Good luck, Yara.'

Yara nodded, then loped out of their cell and into the darkness and chaos without another word. Dutch never saw her again.

Dutch tucked the shank into a pocket and slipped into the corridor. The cell block's main doors weren't centrally controlled, and the other prisoners had started applying themselves to the problem of opening them with considerable vigour. Most, like Yara and Dutch, had little or nothing to lose.

It occurred to Dutch that whoever had shut down the power must also have disabled the backup generators designed for such an eventuality. Clearly someone had thought this through.

She looked around, trying to figure out her next move. A dark mass on the floor of a neighbouring cell resolved into a body, outlined by a growing pool of blood. When you put fifteen hundred extraordinarily dangerous people together in the same confined space for a number of years, she had soon discovered following her incarceration, certain enmities tended to develop. There would be more such reckonings before daylight arrived. Survival meant putting as much distance between her and anyone else who might feel the same way towards her.

Making her way down the corridor away from the main entrance, she found a steel conduit bolted to a wall and rising to the ceiling. One of the skylights looked like it might be within reach, were she to shimmy up the pipe.

It took some effort, but Dutch managed to grip the pipe around its circumference with her hands and knees. After several minutes of steady work, she'd succeeded in climbing all the way up to the ceiling. She rested there for a moment, her skin slick and her leg and arm muscles burning. On any other day the guards would have beaten her unconscious and thrown her into solitary confinement by now.

Gripping the conduit tight with both knees, Dutch reached out with one hand and managed to snag a catch on the skylight. It consisted of about a half dozen panes of strengthened glass, each of which swung upwards independent of the others. Dutch pushed it open with fumbling fingers and gripped the metal edge of the frame.

A roar came from the far end of the corridor, and Dutch guessed the main cell block door had been forced open. She resisted the urge to climb back down and join them. She'd made too many enemies over the last five years for it to be worth the risk.

Dutch grabbed hold of the frame with her other hand as well before unlocking her knees from around the conduit. She hung loose for a moment, then pulled herself up, all the while employing some of the more colourful Russian expletives Yara had taught her. At last she emerged into the night air, straining to pull the rest of her body onto the roof.

She lay there panting for a while, then stood and looked across a flat roof coated in asphalt. A flash of light came from the direction of the main gates, followed by the echoing sound of gunfire. At a guess, the guards were fighting to restore order. From further off came the distant wail of more sirens, this time belonging to police cars.

Dutch searched around and soon located a gutter pipe bolted to the block's outer wall. She worked her way down to the ground before running across an expanse of concrete towards the three-metre high wall surrounding the prison. She crouched in the shadows and listened until she felt sure none of the other prisoners had come this way.

She looked up at the top of the wall and realised, with a rush of despair, that she hadn't thought through how she'd get over it. Could be with all the prisoners milling about at the front gates, or making a run for it, her chances of escaping that way weren't so bad…

Before she could do anything more, Dutch heard an indrawn breath from behind her shoulder.

She started to twist around, the shank gripped hard in one hand, and felt a boot connect with her ribs. She fell backwards, and a fist soon followed, sending her sprawling. The shank went skittering into the shadows and out of sight.

Dutch coughed and grunted, then tried to get up. Her assailant shoved her back down with a boot.

Dutch looked up to see a small, almost grandmotherly woman in late middle-age. She had large white teeth that gleamed from beneath blond hair cut close to the scalp. Anna Dubayev, the Cannibal of the Steppes. She grinned at Dutch, a meat cleaver clutched in one hand.

Dutch stared at the cleaver and wondered how the hell she'd kept it hidden from the guards all these years.

'Oh, *bublik*,' said Anna, 'were you going to leave without saying goodbye to your old friend?'

'I thought I'd wait until we were all a long way away from here, Anna,' Dutch grunted in Russian, her eyes mesmerised by the cleaver. 'Wouldn't want to get myself locked up all over again, now, would I?'

Anna laughed. 'They'll catch us all soon enough.' She shifted the cleaver into her other hand, her smile growing wider. 'This might be the only chance I get to give you the farewell you deserve.'

Dutch glanced past Dubayev's shoulder. 'It's too late, Anna. They've caught us already.'

'Is that the best you can do? How very sad.' Dubayev raised the cleaver above her head. 'You know, I always wondered what you'd look like without any –'

The side of Anna Dubayev's head sprayed outward in a fine red mist before she could finish her sentence. The lid of her remaining eye fluttered for a moment before her body went tumbling to the ground, her thin, greasy lips still twisted in a snarl.

At first, Dutch had been sure the figure creeping up behind Anna must be a prison guard, but on closer observation changed her mind. He held an assault rifle, and had dressed for concealment, in all-black clothing and a balaclava that hid everything but his eyes.

'Dai-Hsi McGuire?' asked the man. To Dutch's surprise, he had an English, not Russian, accent.

'I prefer Dutch,' she growled.

'Whatever,' he said. 'You're coming with me.'

She blinked at him. 'Why?'

The Englishman stared at her. 'Do you *want* to get out of here?'

'It's just that –'

A helicopter passed overhead, sweeping a searchlight across the prison grounds. The Englishman grabbed Dutch by the shoulder and dragged her deeper into the shadows, where a second man, also carrying an assault rifle and dressed for concealment, stood watch.

The Englishman kept pulling her along the side of the wall, the second man following close behind. After about fifty metres he came to a halt next to a black rope hanging down from the top of the wall. Dutch watched as he slung his weapon over one shoulder before rappelling up the rope with consummate ease. He dropped into a crouch on top of the wall and gestured to them to follow.

'You know how?' the second man said to Dutch, gesturing

at the rope with a tilt of his chin, his accent Russian.

'I'm not sure…'

'Just grab hold of it.'

She stared up at the waiting Englishman with considerable uncertainty, but the sound of more shooting from across the prison gave her all the impetus she needed. She gripped the rope in both hands and struggled to ascend the same way the Englishman had, her boots scuffing against the rough bricks, but her muscles felt like worn rags after all the climbing she'd already done.

She felt her grip loosening when the Englishman reached down and grabbed her wrist, hauling her the rest of the way up. Dutch soon scrambled into a sitting position beside him on top of the wall, gasping for breath.

'I'll go back down the other side first,' said the Englishman, 'then you. But please don't try to run away, Miss McGuire. I don't want to have to shoot you.'

'What are you – military?' she asked, still gasping for breath. 'You're not Russian Special Forces, for sure.'

Instead of replying, he scrambled back down the rope to the street outside. The rope's other end came from a winch, mounted on the rear of a decrepit-looking mini-bus. The bus had the name of a children's charity written on one side in Cyrillic.

Climbing back down turned out to be easier, but not by as much as she'd hoped. She dropped the last metre, landing hard. The Russian followed close behind her.

She looked around. A row of warehouses stood on the opposite side of the road, and she could see the dark waters of a river beyond them. Instead of re-winching the rope, the Russian cut it with a knife, discarding it at the foot of the wall.

'Okay,' said the Englishman, turning towards Dutch, 'now we –'

He saw the punch coming and tried to dodge back out of

range, but not fast enough. Dutch clipped him on the jaw with sufficient force to send him stumbling against the side of the bus, the assault rifle slipping from his grasp. She ran, legs and arms pumping, aiming for a narrow gap between two of the warehouses.

The Russian shouted something, but didn't shoot. Her gut told her it wouldn't take her more than fifteen, maybe twenty seconds to swim to the far shore of the river. It meant risking hypothermia, but at least it wouldn't kill her. Or so she hoped.

She heard one of the men come running up behind her. Dutch willed herself to run faster, but exhaustion slowed her. She cried out as hands tackled her from behind, knocking her flat.

'Don't move!' shouted the Englishman, twisting her arms behind her back.

She shoved an elbow back and felt it connect with his ribs. He let out a grunt, and in the next instant an armour-plated elephant danced a waltz on Dutch's spine. Her back arched, her body going into convulsions and her teeth clenching together. She recognised the angry buzz of a Taser.

At that precise moment, staying flat on the ground with her face in a mud puddle seemed like the best idea ever.

'Get the tracker,' she heard the Englishman say.

The Russian grunted and his shadow fell across Dutch. She caught the glint of light from a blade and struggled to lift herself, but her muscles felt like broken rubber bands.

His fingers probed the back of her neck, working their way down to her left shoulder. The blade broke her skin and began to dig deep into the upper muscles of her back. Dutch opened her mouth to scream, but the fingers of his other hand had already clamped themselves around her mouth. A guttural howl escaped from between his fingers regardless as he worked the blade deeper.

When he finally unclamped his fingers from around her

mouth, she gulped air and vomited noisily onto the ground. She coughed and spat, then grunted as the Russian pushed her onto her back. He stood over her with something resembling a ball-bearing grasped between two fingers, his hands sticky with her blood.

'Don't want the Russian authorities following us where we're going, now, do we?' he said.

He threw the ball-bearing away, then, with the Englishman's help, got her back on her feet. Her arms were pulled behind her back and something tightened around her wrists. She was dragged aboard the mini-bus and deposited on the floor at the rear, rows of empty seats on either side of her.

The bus started forward, and Dutch rolled against the iron base of one of the seats. Up front, one of the two men sat on an improvised driving seat made from an upturned bucket, a jacker's plug-in wheel pushed into a hole smashed through the dashboard. Dutch recognised the technique; hacking self-drive cars had provided much of her income as a teenager living on the streets of New Detroit.

The bus kept moving for another half hour. When it finally stopped, the two men dragged her back outside and propped her up against the side of the bus. Dutch saw they were in an empty back-street next to a long, dark limousine with tinted windows. The limousine door opened, and a driver – an actual, human driver, judging by her one brief glimpse of a non-jacker steering wheel – stepped out.

'You run into any trouble?' he asked the Englishman. He wore an expensive-looking dark wool suit, his accent Australian.

'Nothing more than expected.'

'Good.' The driver nodded. 'We should move fast, before they cordon off the whole town.'

They pushed Dutch into the rear of the limousine with the Englishman on one side and the Russian on the other. The limo accelerated with smooth precision, the driver visible through a smoked-glass partition. They made several fast turns that left Dutch appreciative of the driver's obvious skill. Streetlights smeared yellow through the windows, and from time to time she heard the distinctive *thump-thump* of helicopter blades passing overhead in the opposite direction.

The limousine turned onto a motorway and left the town behind, the driver navigating his way in and out of gaps between long trains of self-drive cars. Dutch upped her respect for the driver, until it occurred to her the limo must be equipped with a traffic override. Even so, he clearly had skill.

'Hey,' she shouted through the partition. 'You ever race?'

No answer, although the Englishman made a conspicuous point of placing his Taser on his lap.

Dutch turned to look at him. 'Tell me where you're taking me,' she said in a more reasonable tone of voice, 'and I promise not to cut off your dick at the first opportunity.'

The Englishman favoured her with a small, tight grin. 'You're welcome to try.'

'How about telling me *who* the hell you are?'

The Englishman turned away, staring fixedly out of the window.

She sat back, nothing to see outside now except motorway lights and occasional road signs. Dutch tried to think about what kind of people would be willing to stage a commando raid on a prison in order to break her out, and came up blank.

She could draw some conclusions, though. The only people who still owned manual-drive cars these days were billionaires, politicians and cops. She'd have bet serious money on the window-glass being bulletproof. The chassis and shell were most likely battleship steel, making it less a car than a streamlined tank.

The sky had begun to lighten by the time they turned off the motorway, driving down a narrow country lane and pulling to a halt next to an untilled field. A private jet – one of the new Chinese VTOL's, although she couldn't be sure since all its lights were off – sat in the centre of the field, its engines emitting a low hum.

The driver got out and pushed a gate open before driving the limo up next to the jet. Two men in bomber jackets and armed with RPK's stood guard by a boarding ladder. The driver and the Englishman led Dutch up and into the aircraft while the Russian stayed behind.

Inside, Dutch saw a bar and a cluster of couches surrounding a low table. The couches were upholstered in what looked like authentic kaiju-skin. An elderly Asian man with wisps of white hair neatly brushed against his skull and wearing a dark silk suit with a Mandarin collar sat on one of the couches, a smoothness to his cheeks suggestive of plastic surgery sometime in the recent past. The barest hint of a fading gang tattoo peeked out from beneath one sleeve of his suit.

'A delight to meet you at last, Miss McGuire,' said the old man, his voice still carrying a trace of a Teijouanese accent.

Dutch took a step towards him. 'Wu Changxing,' she said, grinding the words out. 'Are *you* the reason I'm here, you son of a bitch?'

'He's the reason you're out of jail,' snapped the Englishman from behind her. 'How about you show a little respect?'

'I don't care,' she spat. 'Everything I know about him shows he's just as much of a son of a bitch as Strugatsky. Now tell me what the hell is going on!'

The Englishman pushed her onto a couch facing Wu. He made sure she could see the Taser still in his hand.

'Please get comfortable, Miss McGuire,' said Wu. 'I'm sorry about all the subterfuge, but we're in something of a hurry.'

Dutch turned to see the driver bring in the boarding ladder and close the door before sitting on another of the couches. The engines built to a steady roar and the VTOL lifted upwards, the sun rotating past the windows of the jet as it turned. The whine built higher, the acceleration smooth and steady as the jet picked up speed.

'Now tell me what the hell is going on,' Dutch demanded.

'I would prefer to begin with a question of my own,' said Wu. 'Why did you try to rob Strugatsky – hadn't he been paying you well enough?'

'None of your damn business.'

Wu chuckled as he picked up a tablet computer from the table before him. 'According to what I have here, Strugatsky sponsored you in the Devil's Run back in '41 with Jack Burton as your navigator. Eighteen hours into the race, a Spine-back sprayed poison in Mr Burton's face and he died in agony two months later in a Shanghai hospital. Six months after that, you were the getaway driver during a raid on a Moscow branch of Strugatsky Securities that went wrong. I don't suppose there's a connection between those two facts?'

'Strugatsky *owed* me,' said Dutch, her voice tight. 'He owed *Jack*. He wanted Jack in that race, but he didn't do a damn thing for him when he got hurt. There were clinics that could have saved him. He didn't need to die.'

'You were close to Mr Burton,' said Wu.

Dutch said nothing to deny it.

This time, Wu's smile appeared almost human. 'How would you like to race again, Dutch? The next Devil's Run starts three days from now.'

Dutch stared at him. '*That's* why you shut a whole prison down?'

'I had no choice. Any other, more legal way would have taken far too long – not to mention the Russian penal system isn't what you'd call *efficient*. You're here because no one else has taken part in the Devil's Run as often as you have and survived.' He leaned towards her. 'Do this for me, Dutch, and within forty-eight hours I'll have your records expunged. You'll be a free woman.'

She worked her jaw and glared at him. 'No way did you go to this much trouble just to have me race.'

'That's true,' Wu conceded. 'There's something I want you to find for me on Teijouan, before Strugatsky does.'

'We're using the Devil's Run as a cover story,' explained the Englishman. 'Strugatsky has the same objective as us, and he's already putting together a team to go in and retrieve the… items we'd like you to help us acquire. But putting you into the Run is the only way we can do that without alerting him to our plan.'

'They won't let me into the race without a navigator. Unless you can get me some kind of exception like they did for Lucifer Black.'

Wu nodded at the Englishman. 'Harry here will be your navigator.'

'I don't suppose you're going to tell me *what* it is you're looking for on Teijouan?'

'Harry will tell you, but not until the race is underway,' said Wu, a flinty look in his eyes. 'If you succeed in helping us achieve our goal, we'll pay you far more than you'd ever get from winning the race.'

'The Devil's Run isn't a picnic,' said Dutch. 'I need to know more than you're telling me.'

Harry opened his mouth to speak, but Wu raised one hand, dark with liver-spots, to silence him. 'You were very young during the evacuations, were you not?' the old man asked.

Dutch shrugged. 'Sure. Why?' She had a brief mental flash of her father gripping her tiny fist in his, of vast crowds of desperate refugees milling about a port while commandeered passenger ships crammed far beyond capacity steered away from shore.

'I remember Teijouan as it was,' said Wu. 'A proud nation. One that pulled itself out of poverty by its bootstraps. Then came the Rift, and men like Strugatsky, who exploited its misfortune for profit.'

Dutch glanced around the interior of the plane. 'You don't seem to have done so badly out of it yourself.'

'Better that someone like me should exploit Teijouan's misfortune than some *laowai* who knows nothing of our culture or history, yes?'

'If you're trying to appeal to my sense of patriotism,' said Dutch, 'I grew up in New Detroit.'

'Stealing cars and performing illegal modifications on others,' said Wu. 'Part of Teijouan's lost generation. If Strugatsky beats us, he will use what he finds merely to enrich himself.' The old man clenched one liver-spotted hand into a fist. 'Anything found there belongs to *us*. To the people of Teijouan, scattered to the winds though we may be.'

As if, thought Dutch, the money he made from putting drivers in the Devil's Run went anywhere but his own pockets; and he hadn't even answered her question. But if he was serious about putting her back in the race… well, that was a different matter.

'So what happens when I turn up at the starting line, three days after taking part in one of the biggest jailbreaks in Russian history? Isn't somebody going to wonder about that?'

Wu took out a phone and held it up where she could see it. 'One call is all that is required. By the time you walk in front of the cameras, the whole world will believe you were released the day before the jailbreak occurred.'

'And if I say no?'

Wu settled back on his couch and cast a not-insignificant look towards the door of the plane before shifting his gaze back to her. 'As far as the world will know, you died in the riot. But if you say yes, we'll fly straight to Japan for the time-trials.'

That much was clear and unambiguous. 'Guess I don't really have much choice but to say yes,' she said dryly.

All three men relaxed noticeably, and she sensed a sudden shift in the atmosphere. 'A wise decision,' said Wu, looking satisfied.

*Fuck you*, thought Dutch, watching as Harry put his Taser away. The limo driver, who had said nothing since boarding the jet, listened and watched with evident interest. Something in his body language made her think he might be something more than a chauffeur.

'If you're supposed to be my navigator,' she said to Harry, 'I need to know what kind of experience you've got.'

'Harry's a former Captain in the SAS,' said Wu. 'He took part in the mass airlifts from Teijouan back when the Rift first formed. Not to mention he's a veteran of the Second Korean War.'

'I also drove in a couple of cross-continent rallies,' Harry added with evident pride. 'And I reached the finals in the Silk Road Rally, and the African TransContinental. I can handle myself fine on the road, Miss McGuire. You've got no concerns there.'

'Not bad,' said Dutch. 'Did you ever come face to face with any kaiju? I mean the really big, nasty ones like a Spine-back, or a Viper-tail, maybe?'

Harry hesitated a moment. 'I can't say I did,' he admitted. 'But I don't see why it should be any problem. I've made an extensive study of all the current research on kaiju encounters.'

Dutch sucked her lips and thought. 'Tell you what,' she said, leaning towards him, 'I don't drive with anyone until we shake on it.'

She reached out her right hand. After a moment's hesitation, Harry grasped it. 'I think we'll work together very –'

Before he could finish, Dutch reached out with her other hand, took hold of Harry's index finger, and twisted it in a direction it hadn't been designed to go. She heard an audible crunch, and the Englishman's face turned white.

'Jesus!' he howled, yanking his hand back and staring at her with murderous fury. 'You broke my finger, you fucking bitch!'

Dutch sat back with her hands held high before either of

the other two men could react. The driver had stood, his face dark with fury and a second Taser in his hand.

'Take it easy!' she shouted. 'I had to do it for the sake of everyone involved.'

The driver moved towards her, but Wu reached out and stopped him with a hand on his arm.

'The reason you're not taking a walk out of this plane without a parachute,' said Wu, his voice full of menace, 'is because of all the time and energy it took to get you here. But if you can't give me a good reason for what you did, you're about to die, Miss McGuire.'

'I am not going *anywhere* on that island with a navigator who's got no real idea of what he's getting into,' Dutch snapped, hands still raised in surrender. 'And we both know there's a truckload of drivers out there who've gone face to face with Long Tall Sally and worse, and they'd still give their eyeteeth for another chance.' She jerked her head towards Harry. 'This asshole would get us both killed, so if you want me in the Devil's Run, find me a navigator with actual experience of the damn thing. No way they're going to let him navigate with a broken finger.'

Wu's mouth worked for several seconds before he managed to get any more words out. 'A broken finger won't keep him from navigating.'

'He needs to be fit enough to take the wheel from me if anything happens to me,' said Dutch. 'It's in the rules. The race authorities won't even let him take part in the time-trials with a damaged hand.'

Wu's gaze darted towards the driver, who nodded confirmation.

'Fine,' Wu hissed between gritted teeth. 'But do anything like that again and I'll gladly find myself another driver.'

'Christ!' shouted Harry, his expression incredulous. 'You're going to let her get *away* with this?'

Wu glared at him. 'Be quiet, Mr Montrose.'

Dutch sat back and tried hard not to show her satisfaction
.

# ODAIBA HILTON ROOM SERVICE

They banished her to a couch in another corner of the cabin while the three men conferred amongst themselves for the rest of the short flight. The limousine driver bandaged Harry's broken finger, Harry staring over at her all the while with eyes full of murder. But when they touched down at a small provincial airport, Dutch found herself less than surprised when Wu informed her that the driver – whose name she learned was Nat – would be going with her the rest of the way to Japan.

'Where are we now?' asked Dutch, standing at the top of the boarding ladder. All she could see were a few rain-streaked buildings next to a short runway.

'Odessa,' said Nat, following her down.

She glanced back at the VTOL. The pilot had closed the door of the plane and was moving the boarding ladder out of the way. 'What about Wu?'

'He's going somewhere else.'

Nat kept a careful eye on her as he guided her across the concrete to a cargo plane that looked like Russian military surplus, *Wu Changxing International* displayed on its fuselage. She heard a roar of engines, and turned in time to see the VTOL lift up, its nose tipping back before it shot towards the clouds.

Apart from a couple of passenger seats welded to its interior walls, the cargo plane's hold was empty. Nat picked up a shopping bag from a seat and handed it to her. She found it contained Levi's, a white cotton T-shirt, underwear, a leather bike jacket and a pair of boots.

'You shouldn't have,' she said dryly.

'Couldn't have you turning up at the time-trials wearing a prison uniform, now, could we?'

'It wouldn't be the weirdest thing anyone ever wore in the Devil's Run,' she said, staring around the empty hold. 'How long until we get to Japan?'

'Twelve hours.' He stepped towards the cockpit door. 'You'd better get comfortable, because we'll be taking off straight away. If you need me, I'll be up front with the pilot.'

He stepped through the door and pulled it shut, leaving her alone. *Thanks a bunch*, she thought. Even a fold-up cot would have been nice; it wasn't like she'd had so much as a full night's sleep.

She stripped off the prison uniform, balling it up and tossing it into a corner. As soon as she put on the Levi's and T-shirt she felt better, as if she'd grown a new skin. She belted in as the plane started to move. Once they were above the clouds, she folded down the arms of the seats on either side of her and stretched out, the leather jacket balled up for a pillow.

To her surprise, she fell into a long and dreamless sleep, and by the time she woke they were already in Japanese airspace and circling in for a landing at Narita International. She dragged herself over to a window and stared with groggy eyes down at the Shinjuku Line, a broad swathe of destruction several kilometres long that started from the shore before cutting diagonally through the city. It marked the path a Venomosaurus had taken before the Japanese military managed to beat it back into the sea.

A second manual-drive limousine waited for them outside the airport. Nat took the wheel, guiding them through Shinagawa before pulling to a stop outside a Hilton near the port. When he showed Dutch to her room, she found it had a view over the river and Tokyo's Roppongi district.

After five years in a cell with Yara, pretty much everything looked like impossible luxury to Dutch. She even found a second shopping bag on the bed with more clothes, and, beside it, a three-ring binder thick with paper. She flipped through the pages, finding it contained specifications for a Toyota four-wheeler modified for driving in the Devil's Run.

She held the binder up where Nat could see it, then let it drop back onto the bed with a thud. 'What the fuck is this?'

'Specifications of the car you'll be driving.'

She regarded him with horror. 'You cannot be serious.'

'Is there a problem with it? I've seen other racers drive vehicles same as that one on Teijouan. They're rock-solid and built like tanks.'

'Yeah, and how many of the people who drove them survived until the end of the race?'

Nat hesitated. 'Well…'

'Nobody *ever* outran a kaiju in one of those things,' said Dutch. 'Speed and manoeuvrability matter a hell of a lot more than armour-plating or any of that ridiculous shit you see people putting on their race vehicles. Plus, they blow their head gaskets all the fucking time.' She shook her head in violent disagreement. 'If your boss thinks I'm driving one of those things, then he's out of his skull.'

'The time trials are tomorrow,' Nat reminded her, stepping towards the door. 'There isn't time to find another car. And besides, we aren't going there to win, remember? Your job is retrieval. Or would you rather go back to jail?'

*And wouldn't I love to know what it is you're looking for,* she thought, working hard to suppress her anger. 'I'm warning you,' she said, pointing at the binder, 'we go driving around Teijouan in one of these things we've got that much less of a chance of making it back out alive, whatever reason we've got for being there.'

'I'll wake you early so we can get to the racetrack in time,' he told her, stepping over to the door. 'Get some rest.'

She slammed her fist against the nearest wall. '*Fuck* you. I should go out there and steal me something, and I'll bet you whatever I find's going to leave that heap of garbage in the dust!'

His expression hardened. 'You'll stay put. We're still working on how to explain how you got here without having to answer some very difficult questions.'

She sank onto the edge of the bed. 'What's your deal, anyway? You're not some chauffeur. I saw the three of you talking on that jet, and I could see that Wu paid a lot more attention to you than he ever did to that asshole Harry.'

'I'll be next door,' he said, and departed, pulling the door shut.

'You know it's been years since I got behind the wheel of a car, right?' she shouted through the door. 'Maybe I can't drive any more, did you think of that?'

No answer. *Asshole.*

Dutch sighed and ran her fingers across the bed sheets, then realised she hadn't had a shower in a couple of days. She went to the bathroom, investigating the complicated faucets and smelling the soap. Once she got the temperature right, she stripped off and cleaned away the grime and sweat, then changed into fresh underwear and another, identical white T-shirt from the shopping bag; at least whoever had picked her clothes had done their research. Then she went to stare out the window at a skyline she never thought she'd see again.

Something – some subliminal sense born of a billion years of tooth-and-claw evolution – brought Dutch awake in the pre-dawn hours, her heart pounding as if she'd awoken from a bad nightmare. The window stood open, letting in a breeze.

Dutch stared out the window at the neon lights of Roppongi across the river. It had been closed when she'd gone to sleep.

In that same moment, she became aware of a dark-clad figure standing motionless next to the window. Then it moved towards her with sudden swiftness, light reflecting from a long, tapering blade held out at an angle from its hip.

Dutch threw herself off the bed, landing in a tangle of sheets on the floor. The blade whispered past her neck, missing by millimetres. The assassin – for Dutch had little doubt that the intruder intended to kill her – leapt onto the bed. He wore black combats and T-shirt, eyes visible above a patterned bandana pulled up over his nose.

The sword flashed again, swinging down towards Dutch. She jerked back just in time, the blade again whispering past her neck. Without thinking, she grabbed hold of some of the sheets still on the bed and yanked them hard enough the assassin stumbled and fell backwards.

By the time he had leapt back upright, Dutch had run into the bathroom. She had just got the door closed when the blade cut deeply into the wood, its point emerging a few millimetres shy of her nose. She heard the assassin grunting from the other side as he tried – and failed – to tug the blade free.

*Bad move*, thought Dutch. She pulled the door open hard, yanking the sword-handle out of his grasp. His eyes met her for one brief instant before she slugged him hard on the nose, knocking him backwards with sufficient force that his feet became entangled in the sheets on the floor. He landed, arms flailing, on the bed.

Dutch held the door open with one foot, grasped the handle of the sword with both hands and managed to pull it free.

The assassin rolled off the bed and leapt back to his feet, a second, shorter blade grasped in one hand. But not quite fast enough: Dutch brought the longer sword around and rammed its point between his ribs.

He let out an agonised grunt, his eyes wide and full of horror as he staggered back and again fell sprawling onto the mattress. His legs kicked and thrashed, and then he stopped moving, a dark stain spreading out across the mattress beneath him.

The door to Dutch's room crashed open to reveal Nat in T-shirt and shorts, a pistol gripped in both hands and an underarm holster thrown over one shoulder. He stared at the sprawled body on the bed like he couldn't quite make sense of what he was seeing.

'Jesus *Christ*,' he exclaimed, looking back up at her. 'What the *fuck* is going on?'

'He tried to kill me.'

His eyes moved from the blade still gripped in Dutch's hands, to the body, then back again. 'Easy,' he said, raising one hand towards her. 'You can put that thing down now.'

She gave him a tight nod, then let go of the sword as if its very touch burned. The weapon fell onto thick carpeting, smearing it with blood.

Nat switched on the light, staring at the scene before him. His eyes grew wide for a moment, and then he turned to her, pushing the pistol back into its holster.

'You okay?' he asked.

'I'm fine.' She leaned back against the bathroom door, gripped by a sudden chill. 'He came through the window. He must have made a noise or something, because I woke up before he could skewer me.'

'That's a katana – a samurai weapon,' he said, nodding at the sword where she'd dropped it. His gaze moved back to the dead man. 'What is he, a ninja or something?'

'Something like that.' Dutch forced herself to breathe more evenly until her heart rate dropped a little: she was still in fight-or-flight mode. A more urgent need took hold of her and she turned towards the bathroom. 'I gotta pee.'

When she came back out, she found Nat had pulled on some clothes and was busy talking on his phone. 'You're going to have one hell of a lot of explaining to do to whoever owns this hotel,' she said once he hung up.

'The hotel's owned by one of Wu's subsidiaries.'

She let out a weak laugh. 'I should have guessed.'

'Someone's coming to deal with all this mess. And I'm moving you to another room.'

He knelt next to the dead man's body and searched through his pockets, taking care to avoid getting any blood on himself. He found a red envelope and a pre-paid travel card.

'Let me see that,' said Dutch, snatching the envelope from him. She opened it, finding a single sheet of rice paper with intricate Japanese calligraphy. Dutch stared down at it with a powerful sense of unease, then showed it to Nat.

Nat stared at it with a perplexed expression. 'I don't read Japanese.'

'It's from a woman who likes to call herself Madame Muto –'

Nat's eyes grew wide. '*Muto*?'

She squinted at him. 'You've heard of her?'

He blinked like a deep-sea fish confronted by a torch-wielding diver. 'I… guess her reputation precedes her.'

'She owns a bunch of clubs and hostess bars all over Roppongi, but that's a cover for her real business.' She held up the sheet. 'Any time someone pisses her off enough she wants them dead, these get left on their bodies so everybody knows what a mean motherfucker she is. She calls them "death notices".'

That the ninja had been sufficiently lacking in talent he couldn't even kill Dutch while she was asleep suggested Muto's standards had slipped badly since Dutch last encountered her.

'And do you happen to know *why* Muto wants you dead?'

'It's a long story,' Dutch sighed, letting the rice-paper slip to the floor. She found her Levi's and pulled them on. 'I'll tell you some other time.'

Nat tossed the dead man's travel card onto a desk. 'Anyone else coming after you?'

'Knowing Muto, it's entirely possible.' Dutch glanced at the three-ring binder, which still lay on the floor where she'd discarded it. 'She once told me never to come back to Japan, or she'd kill me.'

He regarded her with a sour expression. 'And yet you somehow neglected to inform me.'

She gave him a hard look. 'It's not like I *told* her I'd be coming back. And I'm only here for the duration of the time-trials, right?' Her eyes returned to the three-ring binder and a sudden idea came to her. 'You know, they do say offence is the best form of defence. And unless she's sold it some time in the last five years, Muto has the car I used to drive in the Devil's Run.' She moved closer to him. 'How about we go get it?'

Nat's eyes widened, and he put out a hand. 'You are *not* going to get Wu into a war with some gangster because they've got a grudge against you. We'll increase security until we fly out to Teijouan.'

'But –'

'That's final, Dutch – I don't want to hear one more word about this.' He glanced at the corpse on the bed and shuddered. 'Stay right where you are while I sort out some extra security.'

He left the room and she waited a moment before pushing

her head out into the corridor. She saw Nat standing close by the elevators with his back to her.

Her blood still burned hot and spiky with adrenaline. She pulled on her boots and grabbed up her jacket before she had time to reconsider. Her heart raced like it used to back in her car-jacking days.

She stopped by the door and looked back at the body on the bed, the shorter of the two swords still protruding from his chest. She stepped up onto the bed, took a two-handed hold on the *wakizashi* and tugged it loose, wiping it clean on a pillow miraculously unstained by blood.

Dutch wrapped the blade up in her leather jacket and held it close to her chest as she looked back out into the corridor. There was no sign of Nat, but she could hear him still talking from inside his room next door.

She snatched up the dead man's travel card and headed down the corridor in the opposite direction from the elevators, the soft carpeting blanketing the sound of her footsteps. She hurried down a stairwell, hoping nobody paid too much attention to the *gaijin* woman with a half-concealed sword in her hands.

Two minutes later, Dutch walked out of the hotel entrance and hailed a taxi, the dead man's travel card in one hand.

The Roppongi District hadn't changed that much in the six years since she'd last been there. It still smelled of grilled *yakitori* and hot, damp concrete. She had the taxi – a self-driving pod, naturally – pull up in a narrow alley she had last visited many years before.

In Dutch's experience, Muto's death notices came in threes. The first, left on a target's pillow as they slept, would terrify them into submission. The second arrived with a phial of poison, indicating that the target should do the job themselves rather than endure the awful anticipation of the third, and final, notice, left on their bloody corpse.

That Muto had sent someone to kill Dutch outright rather than warn of her impending doom went to prove how really, truly pissed-off she was. Either that, or the woman's sense of the dramatic had diminished with age.

The taxi trundled away after she had disembarked. People hurried past the mouth of the alley in bright-coloured shoals, heads down to avoid the rain. She located by memory a narrow doorway between a tattoo parlour and the entrance to a hostess club and made her way up tiny, cramped steps to the third floor. She pressed an ear against a door and heard a series of explosions and popping sounds overlaying peppy video-game music.

Dutch slid the *wakizashi* out from under cover of her jacket, then stepped back before kicking the door hard. Its cheap hinges gave way on the third attempt.

The one-room apartment on the other side was tiny and cramped, its walls covered with pictures torn from games magazines and manga books. A heavy-set man in his mid-thirties, naked but for a pair of shorts, stood gaping at her. A computer screen still ran some techno-pop video game, and she saw a bucket under the chair where he'd been sitting. Dutch wrinkled her nose, smelling urine and body odour, and swallowed back a rush of phlegm.

'Fuck me,' she said, stepping towards the fat man with the tip of the sword aimed at his chest, 'aren't you a little old for this, Hiro?'

Hiro staggered back from her, his face twisted up in terror, and almost kicked over the bucket beneath his chair. He raised his hands and made little panicked sounds that caused his jowls to quiver. Then, at last, recognition lit up his eyes.

'Dutch!' he croaked in surprise. 'It's *you*? I thought –'

He caught himself, but not quite in time.

'That they put me in jail?' she asked, coming closer. 'Or that someone killed me?' She lifted the tip of the sword until it touched his quivering chin. 'Which?'

'She – Muto – I –' He gulped hard, moving back up against a wall beside the computer as he struggled to avoid the blade. 'I – I didn't know you were back.'

'Bullshit,' she hissed. 'You're the one who figured out I was back in Tokyo, aren't you?' She nodded at the computer. 'Still her little pet hacker.'

He stared at her. 'What? No, I had nothing to do with that. I mean –' he halted.

She moved the point of the sword down to his belly button. 'Imagine the mess,' she said in a low voice, 'if all this fat and guts got spilled on the floor. What were you about to say, Hiro?'

'No, please.' He made a whimpering sound and dropped to his knees. 'We were friends. You don't need to do anything like that.'

'We were never friends,' she reminded him. 'Who's the guy you sent to kill me in the hotel?'

'Private contractor,' Hiro said in a rush. 'That's all I can tell you. Even I don't know his name – he's one of Miyoko's personal contacts.'

'How did Muto know I'd be in Tokyo?'

'I swear I don't know! She told *me*, Dutch. I don't know where the information came from!'

She felt sure the little shit was lying, but she didn't have time to figure out the truth: not with the time-trials mere hours away. She kicked him hard in the crotch and his face turned purple. He slid onto his side, gasping, his hands reaching down to try to shield himself.

'Tell you what,' she said, staring down at him. 'Your chances of staying alive go *way* up if you tell me exactly what I want to know. Understand?'

He nodded frantically. 'Whatever you say, Dutch.'

She smiled with grim pleasure. 'I want the car.'

He blinked. 'I – what car?'

'You know which one,' she snarled. 'The Coupé. I want to know where she's keeping it.'

His eyes grew round. 'No,' he said, his voice rank with desperation. 'I can't do that. You know Miyoko Muto. Whatever you do to me, she'll do worse if she finds out.'

'Well, since you're such an elite fucking hacker, you'd better make sure she doesn't find out – not unless you want your guts to wind up in that bucket of yours.'

It took a few minutes, and she watched him like a hawk the whole time, but soon enough she had both the address of a warehouse where Madame Muto stored some of her vehicles and the combination number for a safe in which, Hiro rushed to inform her, the Coupé's car keys were locked. She used a bunch of computer cables to tie him up before gagging him with a half-rancid T-shirt she dug out from a pile in a corner. Then she headed back out, the sword once again wrapped up in her jacket, and caught another taxi halfway across town.

On the way, she used the taxi's comms service to send a message to Nat care of the hotel, then sat back, brooding as the city sped by.

She found the warehouse down a side-street in Ikebukuro. Dutch stood next to a noodle stall on the opposite corner from the warehouse entrance, pretending to study the menu, and saw a single guard by the ground-floor entrance. Metal steps above the entrance gave access to an upper floor.

The guard regarded Dutch with suspicion when she walked towards him. She played the naive *gaijin* to the hilt, acting like a lost tourist until he made to push her away. That got her close enough she could pull him off-balance before slamming the heel of one hand into his nose. His head snapped back, and she pushed the attack, driving the back of his head against the wall behind him. His eyes rolled up and he crumpled at her feet.

Muto relied on people being so terrified of her that she never bothered too much with strong security. Her true strength, she had once bragged to Dutch, lay in her reputation.

Dutch dragged the guard inside the warehouse, hoping to hell Nat had got her message. Inside she found a single open space with a metal-floored walkway one floor up; she counted four standard self-driving pods, a vintage Jaguar, and a 1973 Ford Falcon XB GT Coupé with twin V8 engines and a black-and-red paint job. The very sight of it made her throat turn dry and her thighs grow warm with blood.

The Coupé faced towards a roll-down steel door that opened onto the street. Dutch traced her fingers along its hood, full of admiration. Whatever else she might say about Muto, she'd done a terrific job of restoring it after its last race.

She stepped away from the Coupé with great reluctance and made her way up to an office on the second floor. She opened a cupboard and found the safe. She tapped in Hiro's code and it swung open, revealing bundles of cash, bags of white powder, and the keys for the Coupé. She took the keys and left the rest.

Dutch emerged from the office to find a large and muscular-looking Japanese man in a dark suit standing at the other end of the walkway, a Glock automatic aimed at her head.

'Long time no see, Dai-Hsi,' said a familiar voice from down below. 'Why don't you put that sword down and come join me?'

Dutch glanced over the railing to see Muto standing next to the Coupé, surrounded by several more heavies in dark suits with their weapons aimed up at her. Muto wore a shimmering dark dress, her skin pale beneath artfully coiffed hair.

Dutch stood frozen, car keys in one hand and *wakizashi* in the other, and realised she had no choice but to do what Muto said. She bent at the knees and slowly placed the *wakizashi* on the floor, then somehow made it down the steps to where Muto waited without faltering. The heavy with the Glock followed close behind, stooping first to pick up the blade.

'You didn't need to dress for the occasion, Sally,' said Dutch, coming face to face with Muto. She had to work hard to suppress the tremor in her voice.

Muto's eyes were full of glittering fury. 'You will *not* call me by that name!'

'Then *you* can call me Dutch.'

'Fine,' Muto snapped. 'I learned you'd come here right in the middle of dinner with the Malaysian ambassador.' Her fingers stroked the Coupé's hood much like Dutch's had. 'It didn't take much to guess why.'

'I suppose Hiro told you.'

Muto regarded her with a sorrowful expression. 'Oh, Dutch – didn't it occur to you I might have had someone watching the hotel? You were followed the whole way here.'

'All I want is the car,' she said, holding up the keys. 'And then I'm gone from your life forever.'

Muto smiled like a cat that had stumbled across an open bird cage. 'We both know *that's* never going to happen.'

'I think it is,' said a voice from above them.

Dutch looked up to see Nat standing on the walkway she'd recently vacated, his pistol aimed at Muto's head. A door stood open, leading to the external staircase. Four more men spread out on either side of him, all dressed in black bomber jackets and dark jeans, and all, like Muto's men, armed to the teeth.

*And there was me doubting you'd come*, thought Dutch, looking up at him.

Muto's expression didn't change, but her eyes did grow a little wider.

'Dutch,' said Nat, without taking his eyes off Muto. 'I want you to move towards the exit.'

'Not yet.'

A spark of anger flowered in his eyes. 'Dutch…'

Dutch looked back at Muto. 'Like I said, I want the Coupé and then I'm gone.'

'Why should I give you anything,' Muto replied, 'when all I want from you is your life?'

Dutch somehow found sufficient willpower to take a step closer to Muto. 'You owe me.'

Muto stared back in confusion. 'What?'

'C'mon,' said Dutch. 'You're not seriously telling me you forgot about that thing like a giant slug in Lungshan, in the ruins of the old temple?'

Muto's gaze momentarily softened. 'I haven't thought about that in years.'

'I know things turned sour between us,' said Dutch, 'but if you give me back my car, and call off whatever death notices you've got out on my name, maybe we can call it even.'

Just for a second Dutch thought Muto might relent, but then her expression hardened once more. 'No,' said Muto. 'It's too late for that.'

'I *saved your life*,' said Dutch. 'You told me yourself you owed me.' She glanced at Muto's soldiers, sensing they were listening, even while their attention was apparently fixed on Nat and his men. 'Your whole reputation rests on never going back on your word, right?'

'Any debt I owed you was cancelled when you murdered Jack,' Muto snarled. 'For that, I should kill you myself. At the very least, I'd save myself having to pay anyone else to do it.'

'Sure,' Dutch agreed, feeling a thin line of sweat form across her brow, 'you could do that. But word would get around.' She nodded towards the nearest of Muto's men. 'People would talk.'

Muto's nostrils flared with suppressed fury. She stepped towards the heavy still holding the *wakizashi* in one hand and snatched the blade from his grasp.

'Please don't do anything rash, Miss,' said Nat from above.

Muto ignored him, turning back to Dutch with murder in

her eyes, the *wakizashi* gripped tightly in one hand.

'Think about all you'd lose,' Dutch said quickly. 'Everything you've built over all these years.'

With an effort of supreme will, Dutch maintained at least a semblance of calm as Muto stepped up close enough that their noses almost touched. 'It would be worth it,' Muto said in a half-whisper. 'Almost.'

Then she threw the sword down, sending it spinning away with a clatter, and stepped towards the side-exit. 'But don't think this makes us in any imaginable way *even*,' she added, slamming the flat of one hand against a control unit mounted on the wall.

The roll-down door at the other end of the garage shook, then moved upwards, revealing the rain-streaked street beyond.

'Muto…' Dutch managed to say.

Muto stared back at her, her expression full of hatred. 'You have the car. The death notices, however, remain in place. As you said yourself, I have a reputation to maintain.'

Dutch nodded carefully. 'I understand. And thank you.'

'Consider it a last request,' said Muto. Then she snapped her fingers, and her men lowered their weapons. 'Now go burn in hell.'

Muto stepped out through the side-exit, followed by her men. The moment they were gone, Dutch let herself slump bonelessly against the Coupé, trying hard not to think about just how close she'd come to being gutted like a fish.

'Dutch?' Nat called down as he and the rest of his men put their weapons away. 'You okay?'

'I'll be fine,' she said, trying to sound like she meant it. She pulled the door of the Coupé open. 'I'll meet you back at the hotel.'

Dutch slid the keys into the ignition and the engine caught with ease. She let herself sit there for a second, feeling the vibrations roll through her bones, and let her head sink forward until it touched the wheel. Then she brought it back up and drove the Falcon out onto the street, the engine grumbling with restrained power.

She saw a limousine driving away and guessed it was Muto's. Nat and his men meanwhile exited the building, heading for a black unmarked van parked nearby.

Instead of getting in the van with the rest of them, Nat walked over and got in the Coupé beside Dutch. She didn't wait for him to speak, turning the wheel and working the gas pedal. The Coupé shot forward like a greased otter, the acceleration pushing her deep into the leather seating. Something very like an orgasm rolled through her body.

'In any fair and sane universe,' said Nat, 'you would be dead right now.'

She shot a quick glance at him. 'Nice.'

'You have *no idea* how much trouble you've caused, do you? First you disappear, then that… *message*.'

'This car,' said Dutch, 'is my best chance at staying alive on Teijouan.'

She took another glance at him and saw something like resignation. She suppressed a grin and turned onto a busy street where, to her amused shock, the self-drive pods realigned themselves to make way for the Coupé.

She reminded herself it had been Muto's car for a good long while, and she had enough contacts in the police and government to ensure a permanent traffic override. People pointed and stared as they blazed past.

'What the hell's so special about this car you'd risk your damn neck like that?' Nat demanded.

She couldn't help but laugh. 'You're shitting me. Did you even look at this thing? There's no onboard electronics any more advanced than a vacuum tube. Nothing that could get scrambled by Teijouan's d-field.' Dutch guessed there was some kind of fancy override under the hood, but she could strip that out in seconds. 'It's a hundred per cent optimised for the Devil's Run,' she added, tapping the d-meter on the dashboard.

Nat let out a heavy sigh. 'So how come Muto had your old car?'

She grimaced. 'I told you it was a long –'

'I want to hear it. And why you called her Sally. *And* about what the hell happened in Lungshan.'

She gave him a long, sideways look, then turned back to the road. 'Sally Hu's her real name. She's about as Japanese as I am. We ran together when we were kids back in New Detroit, stealing and modifying cars. Then along came Jack.'

'Burton? Your old co-driver?'

Dutch nodded. 'He and Sally were tight – real tight. One time, when she wasn't around, me and Jack kinda…' She waggled one hand above the dashboard.

'I get the picture,' said Nat.

'Anyhow, Sally found out, she and Jack split, we stopped talking and the next thing I knew we'd both got into the Devil's Run on separate teams. Somehow the two of them patched things up and Jack was her first navigator.' She glanced sideways at Nat. 'I came across them in Lungshan on my second Run. Their car had broken down and they were struggling to hold this… *thing* off while they fixed their engine. I helped keep the kaiju at bay long enough for them to get back on the road.'

'You saved their lives.'

'It was a long time ago. A couple of years after that, Strugatsky insisted on putting me and Jack into the same car and… Well, you know the rest.'

'And Muto blames you for what happened to him?'

'Maybe she's got a point,' said Dutch.

'Meaning?'

'Meaning,' she said, 'that I took a risk behind the wheel I shouldn't have, and that's why Jack got hurt – so if she's going to blame anyone it might as well be me. I auctioned this car to raise money for Jack's treatments.' She glanced at him again. 'Muto bought it mostly to spite me, I think.'

Nat shook his head. 'What an unholy fucking mess.'
Dutch nodded. 'Got it in one, man.'

# TWO PRIESTS, A DOCTOR AND A COUNTESS

Nat let her grab a few hours' sleep in his own room with the private security he'd hired posted outside. He woke her later that morning with a hard shove.

'Time to rise,' he said with brisk efficiency, dumping a tray on the bedside table. She sat up, head still groggy, to find he'd brought her croissants and coffee. 'Shower first. You still smell like a prison.'

She stared at him through hair fanned across her face. 'Time?'

'Time to get the fuck up.' He glanced at his wrist. 'I want you in Conference Room Six on the twenty-third floor for a meeting with the boss twenty minutes from now.' He stepped over to the door and wagged a stern finger at her. 'And do *not* be late.'

She showered with a coffee in one hand and a waterlogged croissant in the other, mumbling to herself. She got dressed fast and staggered out the door, where one of Nat's hired goons jerked his chin towards the elevators.

He followed behind her, mumbling into a walkie-talkie. Nat clearly wasn't taking the risk that she might go AWOL a second time.

The conference room turned out to be long, wide and tall enough to play a couple of pick-up basketball games and contained a single, U-shaped table. Nat sat far off at one end, staring at a laptop. When she entered, the minion departed, closing the door after him.

Nat gave her a quick up-down. 'Well, you look like shit.' He nodded to a side table. 'Get more coffee and we'll start.'

She followed his suggestion before taking a seat beside him. She saw Wu on the laptop's screen, seated behind a wooden desk of such vast proportions it looked like it could be taken out to sea were there any place to affix a sail. His gaze shifted towards her as she sat.

'I find myself experiencing regret for releasing you from prison,' he said with a scowl. 'What, precisely, did you think you were doing last night?'

'That's it?' she asked. 'No, *I'm so sorry you were almost murdered by a sword-wielding maniac*?'

'You failed to inform either myself or your navigator you had a price on your head.' A muscle twitched in the man's temple. 'Nor were you meant to abscond in order to *steal a car*.'

'I didn't steal it,' she said in what she hoped was a reasonable tone of voice. 'It's my car.' Not one hundred percent true, not any more, but it felt right to say it. 'So I asked for it back.'

'There may be at least two further assassination attempts,' said Nat. 'I'd like to beef security up further at the Fuji track.'

'Agreed,' said Wu. He looked back at Dutch. 'Any more of this nonsense,' he spat, 'I'll hand you over to the Russians with instructions to chain you upside-down in the main reactor at Chernobyl. Do we understand each other?'

'I promise there will be no further incidents,' said Nat, with apparent confidence. 'Last night caught us all by surprise, but I'll be even more vigilant from this point on.'

Wu massaged his head like he had a bad headache. 'Just get her to Fuji,' he said. 'And for God's sake don't let her out of your sight.'

'So,' said Dutch, once Wu had signed off, 'I get to drive the Coupé?'

Nat drummed his fingers, staring at the blank screen before turning to her. 'It appears so. In which case, I think it's time to talk about your new navigator.'

'You've found someone?'

'Watch this.' He tapped at the computer and a video started running, shot from the perspective of a camera fixed to the hood of a car driving at speed past rusting and long-abandoned vehicles lining the side of a road. She could see one edge of an American Eagle decal on the hood.

Straight ahead of the car were the crumbling remains of a city block, and towering over *that* was a behemoth of a creature with six legs and spines like shards of black glass bristling up and down its back. It was in close pursuit of a second vehicle that combined the extravagant fins of a Lincoln Futura with the sleek, rounded curves of a Phantom Corsair, like some 1950s idea of a spaceship on wheels. The occupants were hidden entirely from sight behind wraparound black windows grey with dust. It shot past the first car, moving in the opposite direction, and disappeared from sight.

The kaiju stared straight down the lens of the first car with eyes like burning coals, and let out a shriek that hurt Dutch's teeth even through the laptop speakers.

Whoever had control of the first car decided, correctly in Dutch's opinion, that their best strategy involved flooring the gas and driving straight under the beast before it had time to react. Kaiju were big and strong, but paid for that strength by being slow and dim-witted.

The camera viewpoint shot towards the kaiju with increasing velocity, and Dutch found herself holding her breath. A leg as wide around as a bundle of tree trunks came thudding down onto the tarmac straight in front of the camera lens and the footage came to an abrupt end.

'Anything look familiar?' asked Nat.

Dutch let out a shuddering breath. No wonder Wu and Strugatsky made so much money out of the broadcast rights. 'The kaiju, or the cars?'

'All three.'

'The kaiju is Long Tall Sally,' said Dutch. 'First sighted in 2025.'

'And the cars?'

'The first one is the Siberian's jeep,' she replied. 'I'd know that hood decal anywhere. The other is Lucifer Black.'

'The Siberian didn't survive that encounter, I'm afraid.'

Dutch looked back at the screen. 'I'm sorry to hear that.'

'Black had overtaken the Siberian a half-hour previous to that encounter. More than likely he doubled back deliberately, knowing there was a good chance Sally might go after the Siberian instead.'

Dutch nodded. It sounded the kind of thing Lucifer Black would do. 'And the Siberian's navigator? He get chewed up too?'

'If he did, he wouldn't be sitting here talking to you.'

Dutch stared at Nat, who favoured her with a thin smile.

'Wait a second – you've been *in* the Devil's Run? How the hell did you survive that?'

He nodded. 'I don't remember any of it. All I remember is waking up in the wreckage hours later.'

'And the Siberian?'

Nat shook his head. 'No sign of him. Most likely he tried to make a run for it and Sally got him. When I came to, the jeep had rolled over on top of me. I figure it kept me hidden from sight. By the time I crawled out from under the wreckage, both Sally and the Siberian were long gone.'

Dutch regarded him with something approaching admiration. 'You were one lucky son of a bitch, coming out of something like that alive.'

He nodded. 'Very much so, yes. I had to hike to the coast and signal to one of the offshore ships.'

All this must have happened while she'd still been in jail, Dutch realised. 'Then why weren't you my navigator in the first place, rather than Harry?'

'Harry's more expendable. I run security for Wu's operations all around the world – or I did, until you forced his hand. Now he's got no choice but to put me in the race with you.'

Dutch pressed a hand against her head and let out a groan. 'You know, if you'd been straight with me from the start, I never would have had to break that asshole's finger.'

'You were too hard on him. Everybody has to race for the first time.'

She scowled at him. 'Doesn't mean I should be the one to babysit them.'

Nat stood. 'We've got a couple of hours before the time-trials start.' He jabbed a finger at her. 'Remember, we are *not* going to Teijouan to win the damn race. It's a retrieval mission, nothing more.'

'Either way, letting me use the Coupé is the smartest decision you've made.'

'And I hope I don't live to regret it.' He glanced towards the door. 'Get yourself more coffee if you need it. We'll 'copter you over to the Fuji Speedway in thirty minutes.'

'No,' said Dutch, standing. 'We'll drive there. In the Coupé.'

Deep frown-lines formed between Nat's eyes. 'We don't have the time.'

'I've been stuck inside a jail cell for five years. I need all the time behind the wheel I can get. Besides, you know how good I can drive.'

She drove them onto the Tomei expressway twenty minutes later, Dutch sliding the Coupé past long trains of driverless cars linked to one another by software. Once again, the vibrations from the twin V8s worked their way up through the leather seating, drumming at her muscles and thighs like a thousand pin-sized Turkish masseurs working in tandem.

Few things, in Dutch's experience, felt as good as being behind the wheel of a car. The wheels felt as if they were glued to the tarmac; now and then she'd catch a glimpse of some round-mouthed face inside a hutch-like pod, there and gone in a blur. She wondered if any of them still remembered what it felt like to take control of your own vehicle – although in truth most had been happy enough to give that privilege up for the sake of zero traffic accidents and safe streets.

She glanced at Nat beside her. 'Now tell me which you'd rather be in when we run into some pissed-off Spine-back that hasn't had its breakfast. This, or one of those redneck Halloween specials with the armour-plating and the gun-turrets or whatever.'

'Fine,' he admitted with clear reluctance. 'Maybe you've got a point.'

'Now tell me why I'm racing with only a few days warning.'

'This thing we're looking for on Teijouan,' said Nat, 'we only discovered existed in the past few weeks. With so little time, we've had to think fast and on our feet.'

The traffic loosened up a little, becoming more sparse. She had a sudden flashback to her teenage years when she'd made a living hijacking self-drive pods and reprogramming them to act as automated drug mules for the Mob. 'So are you going to tell me whatever the hell it is we're looking for yet?'

'As Wu already told you, that's going to wait until after we land on Teijouan.'

She scowled at him. 'Why the hell not tell me *now*? Are you saying you don't trust me?'

'To be honest, Dutch,' he said, 'you haven't given me any reason why I should.'

They made it to the Fuji Speedway in even less time than Dutch expected, thanks to Muto's traffic overrides. It had felt wonderful, but it also, Dutch had to admit, felt too much like cheating.

At Nat's direction, she pulled up outside a military checkpoint where Nat spoke to a guard. They were waved through, and Dutch followed the signs for the West entrance. Despite her cynicism, she couldn't help but experience a certain nostalgic glow at seeing the pit buildings after so many years, all in a line next to the racecourse.

She steered the Coupé past the rusting hulk of an anti-aircraft gun mounted on a plinth near the toll booths in memorial to the Battle of Shinjuku. More soldiers directed them onto a road that led to a cordoned-off plaza behind the pit buildings and the grandstand. Cameras flashed, and people came running towards them. She saw broadcast vans, and reporters speaking into cameras.

Dutch pulled over and turned the engine off. People were moving about with brisk purpose everywhere she looked, some in suits, some in overalls, some talking into phones or yelling instructions to each other.

'Max!' Nat waved to a young man in mechanic's overalls as they got out, then patted the roof of the Coupé. 'Take this to number five.'

'Sure thing,' said the kid, sliding into the Coupé and steering it towards the pit building.

Dutch turned the other way to look at the race track, a long strip of grey tarmac that ran parallel to the grandstand before twisting out of sight. 'What now?'

'The briefing,' Nat told her. 'Then we get to show you off to the press. Any difficult questions, I'll field them.'

The race briefing had been scheduled to take place in a long, low-ceilinged room with strip-lighting beneath the grandstand. She glanced at a race roster posted on a wall, although she recognised no more than one or two names.

A few dozen fold-out chairs had been put out in rows facing a low stage, but no more than a dozen were in actual use. Dutch saw the Countess Philippa Graf von König, wearing a yellow-and-black driving suit, her navigator Wilfred Maur beside her in a buttoned-up shirt, jodhpurs and black leather knee-high boots.

König glanced around at Dutch's entrance and did a double-take. She leaned towards Maur and muttered something. Apart from them, Dutch saw General Hurley, Doktor Elektron, and Dietrich Sokoloff. And if Sokoloff was here, then Lucifer Black was racing, even if, as usual, Black himself remained forever out of sight. The rest were unfamiliar, although a pair of men in priest's cassocks caught her attention.

She took a seat near the back, ignoring the murmurs and over-the-shoulder glances. Andrew Llordes, a race supervisor she remembered from years before, stepped up to a lectern on the stage and shuffled through some notes.

The Countess whispered something to Maur, their heads close together, before turning around in her seat to address Dutch. 'I thought you were in prison,' she said, her voice dripping with familiar condescension.

Dutch flashed her a tight smile. 'Not any more.'

'I assume it wasn't good behaviour that got you out.'

'Didn't they have a riot?' asked Maur with a sneer. 'I'm sure I heard mention of a riot.'

'Dutch got released before the riot broke out,' said Llordes from behind his lectern. He caught Dutch's eye. 'Lucky escape. And welcome back to the race.'

'Thanks, Andrew,' Dutch replied.

'A very *lucky* escape,' added Maur, glaring at her.

Doktor Elektron had also turned to look at her. When he caught her eye, he leered from beneath a domino mask, his open mouth exposing blackened teeth.

'Okay,' said Llordes, shuffling the papers one last time, 'let's get started.'

A satellite image of Teijouan appeared on a screen behind him, much of its centre wreathed in impenetrable cloud and fog. A scale on the map showed the island to be a thousand kilometres in length. In shape it resembled a leaf, broad in the south, but narrowing at its northern tip. Tall mountains ran down its western coast, with equally rugged terrain towards the island's centre.

'Weather's pretty good for this time of year,' said Llordes, 'although there's indications of a typhoon brewing south-east of Japan. It'll hit the East Coast sometime over the next forty-eight hours, but we're not expecting it to interfere in any serious way with the race.' He pointed a remote control at the screen and two red crosses appeared on opposite sides of the island. 'There are two fuel and supply rendezvous, both in the usual locations. I –' he paused as Dutch let out a loud yawn. 'Something you want to say, Dutch?'

'For Christ's sake, why do we even *need* a briefing?' she asked. 'We drive up one side and back down the other side, while trying not to get eaten or stomped on. First to cross the finishing line wins. That's all there is to it.'

'As much as I hate to hear the Lord's name taken in vain,' said one of the two priests, 'I can't deny the young lady has a point.'

'You need to be aware of weather conditions,' said Llordes, regarding Dutch with a no-bullshit look. 'Not to mention major kaiju sightings. You should know this, Dutch. You're pretty much a veteran around here.'

The picture behind him changed to show something that looked like a cross between an armadillo and a porcupine, and big enough to be at eye-level with anyone standing on top of the buildings surrounding it.

'A Spine-back,' Andrew announced. 'Admiral Linares reports multiple sightings of this specific example close to where the course passes through Takau, so take note.'

'Any confirmed kills?' asked a man Dutch didn't recognise. He was big and beefy with an Australian accent, and wore khakis and a slouch hat.

'Four that we know of,' replied Llordes. 'We think it's the same Spine-back that took out Beef Rocket.'

'Man,' said a kid next to Elektron who couldn't be out of his teens. 'I'd like to take that damn beast out myself. I had every one of Rocket's albums. Still can't believe he's gone.'

The kid – who went by the moniker of Kid Atomik, according to the roster Dutch had seen – wore a dark one-piece costume almost as outlandish as Elektron's own black-and-silver affair. She wondered if the kid had ever read Yellow Puma's book about his three years as Elektron's first sidekick; the book had reduced Elektron's reputation to tatters, but somehow he still managed to find new recruits, each more psychotic and unbalanced than the last. She wondered how long Atomik would last before bailing like all the rest.

The screen changed again, this time showing a blurry video of a thing with multiple heads rearing up on trunk-like rear legs. 'I'm sure most of you recognise this as a Screecher,' said Llordes. 'We last observed this particular one fighting a Venomosaurus in the centre of Taihoku. Screechers are the most lethal kaiju so far, with a total of twenty-three known kills to date.' On the screen, the beast lumbered towards another kaiju, almost as big, with silver-grey skin and a long, lethal-looking barbed tail. 'And this is a venomosaurus, of course. They're close behind with a total of twenty confirmed kills.'

'Confirmed kills?' asked one of the priests. 'How many *un*confirmed kills are there, young man?'

'The number of racers who remain unaccounted for outnumber those who are by about three to one, Padré.'

'Where did that footage come from you showed us?' asked the Australian. 'I thought electronics didn't work on Teijouan.'

'All the cars are required to carry cameras mounted front and back that shoot with film stock, since that's unaffected by the island's derangement field. And while we're on the subject, remember that the sponsors require you to keep those cameras rolling as long as possible. The more footage you get, especially if it features encounters with kaiju, the more money you receive after crossing the finishing line.'

'And that's on top of any prize money, right?'

'It is,' Andrew confirmed, pointing the remote control at the screen. 'All right, let's move on.'

The screen changed to show another kaiju loping along a beach past the tumbled ruins of a deserted village. Its tail brushed against a copse of trees, sending them crashing down. It had smooth grey skin like a dolphin, and shark-like fins on its broad back. The focus blurred, then sharpened again, as if taken from a distance. Most likely the footage had been taken from one of the ships that formed a permanent blockade around the island.

'A Gogoro,' said Llordes. 'Twelve confirmed kills in total.' The beast turned towards the ocean, sending up a great spray of water as it swam out from the shore. 'They swim fast and deep, which apart from proving a challenge for the blockade authorities means they can sometimes crop up unexpectedly at different locations around Teijouan. However, this one's been sticking to the area around Truku Gorge, so be alert when you reach that part of the course.'

The screen darkened. 'And that, ladies and gentlemen, is pretty much that. Time trials begin one hour from now. Order of departure is posted in each pit building booth.' He nodded to them all. 'And good luck.'

People stood and began milling about. A couple of caterers had set up a trestle table at the back of the room while Llordes talked, loading it with soft drinks, beer and finger-food. Dutch, famished from a long and sleepless night, piled a paper plate high with turkey sandwiches.

'Dutch McGuire,' said one of the priests, coming towards her.

'Nice to meet you,' she said, shaking his hand. 'Mr…?'

'Iommi,' said the priest. 'Padré Antonio Iommi.' He turned to his companion. 'And this is my navigator, Padré Ian Kilmister. We're great fans of yours.'

'That's… nice.' Dutch put her plate down long enough to crack open a beer and swallow most of it down. 'So… are you real priests?'

Iommi laughed in a good-natured way. 'Quite real, I assure you.'

Dutch felt she was a long way from believing that. 'It seems kind of weird for a priest to be taking part in the Devil's Run. Given how dangerous it is, and all.'

'We're here with the support of the Vatican,' said Kilmister, his voice English and laden with gravel. 'Our mission is to exorcise the kaiju.'

Dutch stopped chewing the chunk of turkey sandwich she'd shoved in her mouth. 'Excuse me?'

'Our car is equipped with rocket launchers modified to fire canisters of Holy Water at any beasts we encounter,' Kilmister explained. 'It is his Holiness's belief that the Rift, and the creatures that emerge from it, are of Satanic origin.'

'You can't be serious. You'll get killed out there!' She looked between them, waiting to see if one of them cracked a smile to let her in on the joke. Instead they gazed back at her with solemn, if polite, expressions.

'Our fate is with God,' said Iommi. 'As is our faith.'

'Then why even take part?' asked Dutch. 'You don't need to be in a race to –' *to throw bottles of fucking water at kaiju*, she almost said. 'I mean, there has to be some other way…?'

'Our initial plan was to fly the Holy Water here aboard drones that could fire it at the beasts,' said Iommi. 'The Holy Pontiff, unfortunately, was unaware that the island's derangement field prevents advanced electronics from functioning within its borders. That leaves us with no choice but to carry out the exorcisms in person.'

'Right.' As far as Dutch could see, they'd be lucky to get to the end of their first day on Teijouan without getting torn apart. 'And of course the only legal way for you to be on Teijouan is if you're racing.'

Kilmister nodded. 'Not to mention that the first prize is over five million dollars – more than enough to rebuild the Saint Fabius Claudius Gordianus Fulgentius School for underprivileged children after the terrible earthquake that struck Mozambique two summers ago.'

Shysters, thought Dutch. Con-men. They couldn't be for real.

'It's for the children, you see,' said Iommi. 'They suffer so very much. And winning would bring such joy to their hearts…' he peered at her. 'I don't suppose you're a person of faith, Miss McGuire?'

'No, I'm not,' Dutch replied through gritted teeth.

'Ah, well. Anyway… we wanted to wish you good luck,' said Iommi. 'And if we don't win…'

'Then it's God's will,' added Padré Kilmister, putting one hand on his co-driver's shoulder. 'But we do *hope* we can win. For the children.' He bowed to her. 'Good day.'

'Assholes,' a voice muttered from Dutch's other side once

the two priests had moved on to their next target.

Dutch turned to see General Hurley standing on her other side.

'It's good to see you again, Fred.' She glanced at the two priests, now deep in conversation with the Countess. 'Those two can't be for real, can they?'

'Hard as it is to believe, they are real. Or so I've been told.'

'I thought you'd have retired by now,' she said.

He grinned. 'You mean retired *again*.' Hurley had spent a few years in command of the naval blockade around Teijouan before surprising everyone by taking part in the race himself. 'You know I couldn't keep away from the island any more than you.'

She grinned. 'Well, circumstances forced me to take an extended break.'

Hurley had the grace to wince. 'I should have thought of that before speaking. But at least you're out now.' He frowned. 'We were all wondering… Why such short notice? I didn't even know you were taking part until I saw you walk into the room.'

'An insane billionaire kidnapped me and told me if I didn't race for him, he'd have me thrown from his private jet without a parachute.'

The General looked startled for a moment. 'Strugatsky?'

'Wu.'

Hurley sighed and shook his head. 'They're both conniving, evil sons of bitches.' He reached out a hand and Dutch clasped it. 'Good luck, Dutch.'

'You too, General.'

'Press in five minutes,' Llordes called out, and people started to make their way out of the room. Nat came over and motioned to Dutch to follow him.

'Stand at the back,' he told her. 'Smile, and don't answer *any* questions.'

She found herself in another part of the building, where a table faced towards rows of seated journalists. Elektron and the Countess were already seated at the table, with representatives of their corporate sponsors standing in a gaggle to one side. Nat pushed her in next to the General, who stood ramrod straight at the back. Cameras flashed, and she saw Nat speaking to a member of the Speedway's security.

The drivers spent the next twenty minutes answering questions. A lot of them were aimed at Dutch, but Nat fielded every last one with practised ease, giving them answers that added up to very little real detail at all.

'Well, at least it was mercifully brief,' he said after they had finished and were on their way back out of the room. He glanced at his wrist. 'We've got thirty-five minutes until the handicaps start.'

'I haven't had a chance to see how the Coupé looks under the hood,' said Dutch. 'I need to strip out any modifications Muto put in there or I'll risk disqualification.'

'About the handicaps,' said Nat, as they walked side-by-side to the pit building. 'Mr Wu wants you to pull back. Don't try to come in first.'

She turned to stare at him. 'Why the hell would I do that?'

'Once again, you're not in the race to win.'

'Even so, you can't expect me not to –'

'We don't want the attention,' he said. 'Let someone else get the headlines. You don't have to come in last – a middle ranking should be about sufficient.'

Her nostrils flared. 'You're asking a lot of me, Nat.'

'Nevertheless.'

She looked him square in the eyes for long enough to see he wasn't going to back down. 'Fine.' She flexed her knuckles and pressed her hands together, fighting down frustration. 'Let's get this the hell over with.'

She made her way alone towards the pit buildings, a row of garages situated beneath the grandstand. When she entered the garage assigned to them, she found a familiar figure kneeling beside the Coupé and peering inside the wheel-well.

'What the hell are you doing?' she demanded.

Doktor Elektron started, then gave her a lopsided grin. His one-piece suit glistened with custom inlaid electronics, a stylised silver lightning-bolt angling down from his left shoulder before terminating at his right hip. The eyes behind the ridiculous little domino mask he always wore were blue, and a little too bright. His dark hair lay flat and greasy against his forehead.

'Dutch,' he rasped. 'It's great to see you back in the game.' He stepped towards her, extending one gloved hand. His costume creaked as he moved, the circuitry flashing silver beneath the overhead lights.

Dutch stepped back and grabbed a wrench from a worktable. 'Stay the hell back,' she yelled, swinging the wrench in a wide arc. 'What the hell were you doing there?'

'Nothing,' he said with feigned shock. 'I didn't even recognise your old car at first.' He glanced at it. 'Sweet ride, Dutch.'

'What the hell?'

Dutch glanced around to see Nat had walked in.

'I found him in here by himself when I arrived,' said Dutch. 'He'd been doing something down by the front right wheel-well.'

Nat stepped past her and up close to Elektron. 'Either tell me what you were doing, or I'll knock your teeth out through the back of your skull.'

'Hey,' said Elektron in an aggrieved tone. 'You know we're allowed to check each other's cars out before a time-trial.'

'Under supervision,' Nat reminded him. 'And you were here alone.' He looked to Dutch for confirmation and she nodded. He reached a hand towards Elektron's shoulder. 'So why don't you –'

'Nat,' Dutch shouted, 'don't!'

Too late: Elektron grabbed hold of Nat's wrist with both gloved hands, pulling him close. Nat gasped, his jaws clamping together in a rictus grin. A faint smell of ozone filled the garage. When Elektron let go, faint blue sparks jumped from the palms of his gloves.

Nat slumped to the floor next to the car. Dutch stepped past him, swinging the wrench with such vigour that Elektron retreated with haste.

'I acted in self-defence!' Elektron screeched. 'And that wrench is metal, you idiot.'

Dutch swung the wrench again, then moved to one side and pointed to the exit. 'Get the fuck out of here before I knock your brain out of your ass. *Now.*'

Elektron glared at her, then darted past her and out through the door. As soon as he'd disappeared from sight, she dropped down next to Nat and helped him back up.

'What –' he grabbed hold of the side of the car to keep himself upright '– the hell happened? Those gloves –'

'You're kidding me. It's *Doktor Elektron.* That's like his *modus operandi.*'

He coughed and stared at her with glazed eyes. 'I guess I forgot.'

'He used to run around New York beating up muggers. These days most people would be cheering for the muggers to beat *him* up.'

Nat swayed as he stood upright. 'Okay,' he said with a shuddering breath. 'We need to take a look at the car, see what the little shit did to her.'

Dutch grabbed a torch from the same place she got the wrench and peered inside the interior of the wheel-well. 'If he planted anything, I don't see it.'

'Seems to me we caught him before he had a chance to plant anything at all. The question is, why do it?'

She looked up at him. 'Muto said there were still two outstanding hits with my name on them.'

He stared at her. 'You think Elektron's capable of murder? He's a creep, but I didn't have him pegged as a killer.'

'Elektron's been on the skids for a long time,' said Dutch. 'He might be capable of anything, if it gave him a chance at coming first in the Run.'

Nat stepped towards the door, still looking pale. 'I'll go let Wu know we're looking at threats of sabotage on top of potential assassination.'

'Aren't you going to tell the race administrators?' asked Dutch. 'It's possible we could get him kicked out of the race altogether.'

'Except then there'd be an investigation,' said Nat, pulling the door open. 'And if Elektron does turn out to be connected to Muto or anyone else, it could open up a whole can of worms we'd rather stay unopened until we've finished our business on Teijouan. After all,' he added, 'the point is for us to *avoid* drawing attention to ourselves.'

Nat returned a few minutes later with six mechanics who near as damn stripped the Coupé down to its chassis and back up again and even took out Muto's traffic-pacifier while they were at it. They found nothing, but it did little to settle Dutch's unease. Then they rolled the garage door up, letting in the morning sun and the noise of the crowd gathering on the grandstand above.

She and Nat were last on a randomised schedule of trial participants posted on the wall of each garage. She stepped out into the sunshine and watched the Australian driver, whose name was Vishnevsky, roll his enormous vehicle up to the starting line. An amplified voice boomed out his statistics, history and betting averages. Vishnevsky was something of a mystery, she learned, with questions around his origins.

Vishnevsky's vehicle leaned towards the tank end of the spectrum, being a modified vintage Oshkosh Tactical Protector that looked more suited to gunning down insurgents in some bombed-out city than racing. It rumbled forward once the flag came down, accelerating faster than Dutch thought such vehicles could. She stepped up to the side of the race-course, watching as Vishnevsky and his navigator threaded their way through a forest of girders pushed into the race-track at different angles before disappearing from sight. A few moments later she heard screeching tyres, followed by the bass thump of an explosion, and a huge cheer from the grandstand audience.

'What's Vishnevsky's deal?' Dutch asked a mechanic standing nearby. 'Is the big game hunter look just some kind of shtick?'

'He's the real deal, a kaiju-hunter,' the mechanic replied. 'He killed a Viper-Tail two years ago and sold the skin for something like thirty million dollars.'

Dutch shook her head in wonder and watched the rest of the contestants drive their time-trials, most often returning with scorched paintwork. Lucifer Black clearly still favoured the flying-saucer-on-wheels look for his current ride, which combined 1960s retro-futuristic styling with fuck-you armoured tyres. The windows, as usual, were tinted one-way so you couldn't see anything inside.

Armoured or not, Black crossed back over the finishing line with two of his tyres blown. Dutch watched mechanics swarm over his weird-looking car like fire ants descending on an injured rodent. Black's identity had remained a mystery for years; no one had ever set eyes on him, and no one had even seen him getting into or out of his car. Some rumours claimed the vehicle was in fact remote-controlled, using secret technology that could operate within Teijouan's d-field. Like many, however, Dutch suspected Black's "representative" Dietrich Sokoloff was the real person behind the wheel.

'Ready?' asked Nat, appearing by her side. He'd changed into a dark blue racing-suit. Dutch, by contrast, intended to race in her street-clothes, as she always had.

'As I'll ever be,' she said, brushing her hands down her jeans. Her palms felt sticky and damp. She felt more nervous than she'd thought she would; it had been a long time after all.

They walked back over to their garage, where engineers and mechanics, under the supervision of Nat's hired security, finished performing last-minute checks on the Coupé and fuelling it up. She felt her heart thud the way it always did before a race, a steady thrum that left her mouth gritty and dehydrated. She got in behind the wheel, Nat sliding into the passenger seat beside her.

She strapped in and guided the Coupé out into the open air. The grandstand appeared to be packed to capacity, and as she pulled up at the starting line, she saw even more people in their thousands scattered across grassy slopes rising up on either side of the race-track. She had a fleeting mental image of a sniper crouched up high amongst the crowds and pushed the thought away.

The countdown began, banks of TV cameras swinging around to focus on them. She focused on her breathing, hands firm on the wheel.

Then the flag came down, and the tyres span against the tarmac, propelling them forward. They hit the first turn, and she eased back, but not too much.

'I heard someone say there's a lake of fire right after the girders,' Nat informed her.

She grunted an acknowledgement. The girders, each six metres long, had been driven into the race-track at different angles. There were a few narrow gaps, but she managed to slalom the Coupé through them without losing too much speed.

*Screw not winning*, she thought, one hand on the wheel and the other on the clutch. A savage grin stole onto her face as the speed built up again.

The next turn brought them in sight of a ramp. Light blossomed on their right as they approached, burning oil spreading across a pool on the ramp's far side. By the time the front wheels hit the base of the ramp, the flames rose a dozen metres into the air.

They drove up the ramp, and for a long moment the Coupé was airborne, passing through the flames. They landed hard on a second ramp, knocking the wind out of Dutch.

They rolled back down to the ground and Dutch took the next bend fast, twisting the wheel hard. The Coupé slid sideways into a long, straight stretch and she floored the gas.

'The fuck?' Nat shouted. 'Are you trying to *win*?'

'Fuck you,' she yelled back. 'You don't like it, *you* drive the damn car.'

They came to another bend followed by another long straight stretch of tarmac Dutch didn't trust one tiny bit. The race organisers were notorious for inventing brand new obstacles for each year's time-trial with what Dutch always imagined to be sadistic glee. The time-trials alone were dangerous enough that every couple of years someone wound up going home in a wooden box without ever reaching Teijouan itself.

Straight ahead, Dutch saw what looked like steel plating laid over the track. As they approached, the steel plating came apart, separating into two halves that rose to reveal a pit dug deep into the ground.

Something huge shouldered its way up and out of the pit; something with multiple legs, chitinous skin, a long, whiplash-like tail and a pissed-off expression.

'Is that –?' Nat started to say, and then the beast was upon them.

*A kaiju,* he'd meant to say. But by the time the thing had climbed all the way out of its hidey-hole, he was too busy screaming to say much else that was coherent. It was one of the lesser kaiju species, being not much larger than a typical mid-range house, but in some ways that made it more dangerous. The small ones moved faster and were smarter.

Somewhere in the back of her mind Dutch wondered who'd caught it, and what process had led them to think *hey, maybe we should chain it up in a hole in the middle of the Fuji race-course.*

Dutch knew she had no choice but to barrel on through. She maintained her speed, noting that the creature was at least restrained by battleship chains wrapped around its extremities.

The creature raised a tail like a scorpion and leapt towards them in a manner that made it clear that the chains were, nonetheless, quite lengthy. Dutch pushed in the clutch and hit the brakes hard, spinning the wheel as far as it could go. The car skidded in a circle until it faced in the opposite direction.

'Christ!' Nat shouted in disbelief. 'You're *facing the wrong way.*'

While she performed this manoeuvre, Dutch glanced in the rear-view mirror and saw, as she had anticipated, that the kaiju had begun to run towards them with even greater speed, believing they were about to flee. Then she put the car into reverse, driving straight under the creature and between its legs before it had time to react.

'That's my signature move, asshole,' she screamed back at Nat.

She kept the Coupé moving backwards, so that they had a good view of the kaiju as it tried to reverse direction. It got tangled in the chains and bellowed its frustration, its long jaws snapping as they accelerated backwards down the race-track.

'And fuck you too,' yelled Dutch, performing the same manoeuvre to bring them the right way around.

She glanced sideways at Nat, who looked shellshocked, his lips set in a thin line. 'When the hell did they start putting *live kaiju* in the time-trials?'

'I think this is the first time,' he replied, his voice small and still.

Everything else the racecourse threw at them felt like a Sunday afternoon drive by comparison. What the Coupé lacked in armour-plating, it made up for in all the agility and speed Dutch had promised. Before long they crossed the finishing-line and the flag came down. Dutch exited to cheers and heard the race commenter announce that they had, indeed, raced the course faster than anyone else.

'Don't look so glum, sport,' she said to Nat as they got out of the car. Engineers and mechanics swarmed around the Coupé. Dutch felt giddy in a way she hadn't in years.

'I told you not to –' He stopped and closed his eyes, his jaw set tight.

'Not to win?' She laughed throatily. 'My ass.'

# TEIJOUAN SECURITY ZONE

The next day, at dawn, Dutch boarded a Chinook along with the rest of the drivers and their navigators and flew fifteen hundred kilometres south-east to the former island-nation of Teijouan – except for Lucifer Black who, as usual, insisted on riding inside his car while it was choppered in separately. She saw the South China Sea far below, and the outline of one of the battleships that formed the blockade. Nat sat beside her, back in his deep-blue racing suit and still monosyllabic. He'd hardly said a word to her ever since she made the terrible mistake of winning the time-trials.

Which was fine with Dutch. She spent the trip flicking through a copy of Kaiju Spotters Monthly she'd found discarded near the grandstand until the island hovered into view.

A light mist covered the ground when they landed at the

Security Zone, a flat spit of low-lying sandy terrain at the very southern tip of Teijouan, a few hundred metres wide and walled off from the rest of the island by a six metre-high steel fence with guards patrolling along the top. Heavy artillery guns poked their long barrels over the fence in the hopes of deterring any inquisitive kaiju that wandered too close. A road passed beneath a portcullis-style gate set into the fence, coming to an end on a low rise near a jetty.

The road had served as a starting point for the Devil's Run since the race's inception. A two-story concrete shell that had once been holiday apartments served as a once-a-year temporary headquarters for military authorities who busied themselves protecting the racers and their attendant mechanics, along with the press and support staff, for the three days the race was expected to last. A dozen speedboats sat moored at the jetty in case the need for a quick getaway presented itself, and when Dutch disembarked from the Chinook she saw journalists and photographers mingling with race officials and military. Several US Navy cruisers sat a couple of miles offshore, their guns also pointing north.

'Hey,' asked Vishnevsky the kaiju-hunter, coming abreast of Dutch as she moved away from the 'copter. He had to shout over the noise of the rotor blades. 'Where are our cars?'

'Coming in now.' She pointed towards a huge Russian-built Mi-26 landing at that moment.

He touched the brim of his hat and grinned. 'Good to know.'

He headed for the Russian cargo chopper at a brisk place and she followed in his wake. By the time they got there, Vishnevsky's Oshkosh had already been brought down the ramp. Lucifer Black drove his own vehicle out into the sun, unseen as always behind his tinted windows. He revved his engine and span his ride through a couple of turns that kicked up sand and dirt before pulling up close by the starting line.

Elektron's Peterbilt semi-truck came down next, and Dutch noted he'd mounted a pair of jet engines on its rear bed. The Padrés had, like the Siberian long before them, picked a souped-up vintage US Army jeep for their ride – a wise choice, in Dutch's experience, given such vehicles required little to no extra modifications to protect them from the effects of the derangement field.

Countess König, by contrast, had chosen a T-model Mercedes Benz – not the fastest car, but sturdy as hell and not given to breaking down in tight spots. General Hurley had picked a Toyota Hilux – fast, manoeuvrable, tough, able to deal with a variety of terrains, and hence popular with insurgents and terrorists everywhere.

She waited until they wheeled her Coupé down the ramp, then supervised as engineers fixed brackets to the hood and rear to support a pair of film cameras. Any footage they obtained – assuming they survived to deliver it – would be edited and broadcast, streamed and displayed around the globe on an endless loop. The boot and rear racks had been stocked mid-flight with the supplies she'd requested – bottled water, survival gear, a repair kit, spare ammo and rockets, enough protein bars to last a week and a spare tyre mounted on the boot.

Nat came over to find her. 'Everything good?'

'So far.' Once the engineers were done, she pulled the Coupe's door open and looked in the back, where space had been made for weapons racks. She nodded with approval, seeing rifles of different calibres, along with an assortment of handguns, numerous boxes of ammo, and a pair of shoulder-fired rocket launchers.

'Not bad,' she said, standing back up. 'Now all we need to worry about apart from giant hungry monsters that want to eat us is a couple of dickbags out to kill me.'

'Maybe they're waiting to see if you survive the Run first,' Nat suggested.

She gave him a pointed look. 'Or maybe we could ask Elektron if Muto hired him to kill me.'

Nat shook his head. 'No way he's involved with Muto.'

'What makes you so sure?'

'I've been looking into Elektron – he's received a lot of warnings from race officials over the past couple of years. Based on what I've been hearing, it's far more likely he meant to sabotage the car to keep us out of the race.'

'Then there's something else I've been wondering,' said Dutch. 'How did the first guy Muto sent to kill me know I'd be in that hotel? Or Muto know I'd be arriving?'

'Good question. If you find out, let me know.'

'Before I went to the warehouse to get the Coupé I paid a visit to a guy called Hiro who does all of Muto's computer hacking. He said Muto hired the ninja, but if she did, it would have to have been before we even landed in Japan. My guess is Hiro found some way to hack into Wu's communications. There's no other way she could have known.'

'That would be worth looking into,' Nat agreed, taking out his phone. 'I'll get his tech people onto it.' He paused. 'Maybe it's worth checking the Coupé over again, a second time.'

'There something worrying you?'

'You said it yourself – there are two people out there who want to kill you. Elektron's one thing, but there's just one of him, and we can't rule out any of the other contestants. Plus with all these engineers, mechanics, race support staff and the rest, there's any number of opportunities for someone to try to sabotage or hurt us.'

'Do we have the time?' she asked sceptically. 'We won the trials, so we'll be the first over the starting line.'

A smile curled one corner of his mouth. 'They decided to flip the order of departure this year and put the team with the worst time in pole-position.'

Dutch swore. 'You mean we'll be the *last* to leave?'

'Yeah, but think about it. It'll give us a few extra hours to check the Coupé over.'

Dutch sighed and stripped off her jacket, throwing it on the roof of the Coupé before cracking open the boot and fetching the toolkit. 'Then I guess now's as good a time as any to get started.'

Nat started to take off his own jacket, and she gave him a look. 'I think you'd know by now I work better on my own when I have a choice.'

He gave her a sharp look, then shrugged his jacket back on. 'And there was me about to give you some advice on teamwork.'

Dutch checked over the engine, chassis, drivetrain, ignition system and tyres for any signs of sabotage. She felt a sour sense of unease when she found something.

'Someone cut the fuel line,' she said a while later, handing Nat a rubber hose. A tiny incision had been cut in it. 'It's not enough to stop us – at least not straight away.'

He nodded, his face grim as he turned the hose in his hands. 'But enough to bring us grinding to a halt a couple of hours into the race and stranded in the middle of nowhere. Nice.'

'Which would make us a sitting target not just for an assassin taking part in the race, but for any kaiju that happened to be in the vicinity.' She glanced towards Elektron's Peterbilt semi. 'Look, the one person we know who's been acting in a suspicious manner is Elektron. I still think we should –'

'No,' he said abruptly. 'We are *not* making an official report.'

'But –'

'I told you, it risks exposing our real reason for being here – and that's final.' He looked hard at her. 'Understand? If he causes us any more trouble, I can deal with him.'

She watched him walk away, then threw the cut hose to the ground in disgust. She thought about going to find Elektron herself and wringing his scrawny, foul neck, but she had a sense that would put her on a fast track back where Wu found her.

*Hold it in, girl*, she told herself, fighting down the anger before it erupted and took control. *Save it until you need it.*

A little while later, she paused from putting in a replacement hose to watch Vishnevsky the kaiju-hunter trundle up to the starting line. Now they'd flipped the race order, he'd be the first to depart, having come last in the time-trials.

Rapid-fire, borderline-hysterical commentary came, as ever, from Wayne Wilson, broadcasting from the flat roof of the command centre-*cum*-holiday apartments. Wilson had covered the race since its inception and had the demeanour of a radio DJ permanently on the brink of an apocalyptic nervous breakdown.

The sun rose higher, and the day grew hotter. She tried, as she often had in the past, to summon up more memories of Teijouan from when she was young, but all she could find was that one moment on the docks, clutching her father's hand and looking up at him and seeing the thick red curls of his beard. It was hard to be nostalgic for a place you barely remembered, if at all.

She cracked a beer and sat on the hood of the Coupé and watched the two Padrés take their turn at the starting line. General Hurley and his navigator came next. Then Lucifer Black, the engine of his black and red vehicle growling like it was alive.

The flag came down, and Black shot towards the raised steel gate in the security fence, accompanied by Wilson's frenetic rambling and stuttering rock music blasted through speakers.

After Black's departure, Countess König was next. Dutch felt an old and familiar excitement grip her. Her own turn would come before long.

She found one of Nat's security team and got him to keep an eye on the Coupé while she took a leak and went to get something to eat in a tented mess hall. She was on her way back out of the tent with a burger and fries when she heard a roar of engines and raised voices.

People came swarming out of the tent behind her to see what all the fuss was about. Dutch cast a wary eye towards the Coupé, saw the security guard still standing next to it, and decided to find out what was going on.

Instead of some kaiju emerging from the sea, as she'd half-feared, Dutch saw six Zodiac semi-rigid motorboats come powering up to the shore. Each carried about a dozen people, all carrying protest signs or shouting through loudspeakers.

Soldiers moved to intercept them, but there were too many protestors wading ashore for them to cope with – not to mention that every news camera in the Security Zone had turned around to film their arrival.

'Hey,' Dutch asked one of the mess cooks, standing watching the approaching Zodiacs with a greasy spatula in one hand, 'is that Adam Lin?'

The kid nodded. 'Sure looks like it.'

Lin's beard and ponytail appeared a little greyer than Dutch remembered. He strode up the beach, his trouser-legs damp with saltwater, waving to the other protestors to follow.

They came charging up in his wake like an invading army from the sea, holding their signs up high and chanting and yelling anti-race slogans. Some of the signs read *Teijouan for the Teijouanese!* Lin made towards the starting line, lifting a megaphone to his lips as he walked.

'We have a right to protest!' he shouted, his voice booming across the flat plain. 'The Devil's Run is a travesty. The people of Teijouan demand a say in everything that happens here. Instead of funding research to reverse the Rift, foreign billionaires use it to make themselves even richer! We should be –'

A response came in a sudden wave of feedback. 'Ladies and

Gentlemen of the press,' bellowed Wayne Wilson, sounding twice as loud as he had moments before, 'if you would *please* direct your attention to the starting line, Doktor Elektron is set to blast off into the far reaches of the unknown!'

Elektron, up high in the cabin of his semi, slammed his horn. It blared out across the shore like the anguished moan of a lecherous dinosaur. Wilson kept up his patter, working hard to drown out Lin.

The soldiers now formed themselves into a cordon between the protestors and the starting line. Dutch looked out to sea. A rusty freighter sat two or three miles offshore, one of many such that resupplied the blockade. She guessed Lin must have bribed its captain to ferry them up close to the Security Zone.

'Doktor Elektron!' bellowed Wilson, 'scourge of muggers and thieves, rescuer of little old ladies, but let's not talk about that tell-all book by his former sidekick, not unless you want him to grab you by the balls with those electric gloves of his!'

This got scattered laughter from the press, and Elektron mouthed something inaudible in Wilson's direction.

'You cannot keep sending people to certain death in the service of entertainment,' Lin responded, his voice barely audible over Wilson's rambling. 'The derangement field alone represents a unique opportunity to study a phenomenon that still defies our understanding –'

'Let's start the countdown!' Wilson shouted into his microphone. 'The flag is up! Doktor Elektron gets ready for his seventh Devil's Run – he's easing off the brake, aaaand…'

The starting pistol fired, and the flag came down again. Elektron's semi-truck shot forward, aided by the enormous rockets mounted on its rear bed.

Ahead, the gate lifted to let him pass through the security fence. By the time Elektron's truck reached it, it had become shrouded in flame and smoke. *All flash, no grit*, thought Dutch.

Lin and Wilson competed for a while longer, but it soon

became clear Wilson had won by virtue of more powerful amplification. Dutch finished her fries and watched from beside the Coupé while the rest of Lin's people settled in for the long haul, chanting and raising signs where they knew the cameras could see them. A few had already pitched tents close to the shore. Lin had always been a canny operator in Dutch's experience; every time he and his protestors found a way onto Teijouan, viewer figures spiralled upwards. She suspected that was why security was never quite tight enough to keep him out.

Then, at last, came her turn.

Nat appeared from the direction of a comms tent where he'd spent most of the day conferring with Wu by remote link. They nodded to each other without speaking and got inside the Coupé. Dutch placed her hands carefully on the wheel and worked at keeping her breathing shallow and even, her mind a storm of elation and panic. Once they were past the fence, they would be on their own.

Across the Security Zone, the gate slid upwards like the blade of a guillotine.

'Dutch McGuire, imprisoned for life in Russia, but free again to drive in the Devil's Run!' Wayne Wilson screamed into his microphone. 'McGuire is one of the few people to survive seven – count them, *seven* – consecutive Runs, but has never once come in first place. Will *this* be the year that turns her into a surefire winner? Or is her luck going to run out like it has for so many others before her? With so much money hanging on this year's race, you have to wonder what she should be more scared of – hungry kaiju, or her fellow drivers. But after that stunning win in the time-trials, all bets are off. Whichever way the race goes, this girl has nothing to lose!'

Dutch peered out through the windscreen at Wilson up on his perch on the roof of the apartment block, surrounded by sandbags, radio techs, TV cameras and microphones. She wound down the window and gave him the finger, raising it high to be sure he could see it. He looked her way and responded to the gesture with a grin and a wave.

'That's the spirit!' cried Wilson. 'I've got no doubt Dutch McGuire and her navigator are in with a chance this year. Their Ford Falcon Coupé is a thing of beauty, ladies and gentlemen, real old-school – and now they're heading for the starting line. And the countdown has begun! It's a clear and sunny day, and reports show that the coast road is quiet. Even the d-field is showing low levels of activity for this time of year. We'd better hope it stays that way for our live transmissions from the blockade! But should we lose signal, rest assured we'll get as much as we can on film and ship it to the technicians waiting on our support vessels. Oh! And here it comes… three… two… *one*!'

Dutch worked the gas. The wheels shrieked against the tarmac, the Coupé fishtailing for the briefest moment before it sped up hard towards the fence and through the gate.

# GUNS, CARS AND KAIJU

Beyond the Security Zone lay nothing but ruins and highways that were crumbling apart with no one brave or foolhardy enough to maintain them. The fence receded from view behind them, Nat unfolding a paper map and spreading it across the dashboard. Dutch glanced towards it, seeing dozens of tiny corrections showing where the road had become blocked or crumbled away entirely, along with a plethora of potential detours.

'Christ,' Dutch muttered, returning her attention to the road, 'five years makes a lot of difference, huh?'

Nat peered ahead, then back down at the map. 'What do you mean?'

'Last time I drove here, I kept the pedal to the metal for the first fifty, sixty kilometres of the Run.' She swung them around and past bushes sprouting from the broken tarmac. 'The road's gone to shit since then.' She nodded at the map. 'How long before we reach Takau?'

Takau was a small city further north. 'Couple of hours, factoring in detours.' He studied the map. 'Says here sections of the coast highway showed signs of slipping into the sea during the last race. That might delay us.' He looked back up and frowned. 'Hey, is that smoke up ahead?'

'Wondered when you'd notice.' A dark smear rose into the sky from behind hills several kilometres to the North. 'Keep your eyes out for anything that moves,' she added, tightening her grip on the wheel.

They passed a garage collapsed on one side, a fading sign in Chinese still about readable. Dutch glimpsed the ocean through tall bushes that grew wild alongside the highway. She saw that a blockade ship lay anchored a mere two hundred metres from the shore – close enough its Captain risked getting his onboard electronics screwed up by the constantly fluctuating derangement field. Chances were he considered the risk acceptable: camera crews on board were undoubtedly tracking them at that moment and uploading the video to an audience numbering in the hundreds of millions.

Nat tapped the d-meter mounted on the dashboard. 'Reading's climbing.'

The ground on their right grew steep, becoming tall hills coated with dense forest. Dutch steered past several rusting vehicles abandoned on the highway close by a former evacuation point, and glimpsed the rusted-orange hulk of a former rescue ship keeled over on a beach.

She glanced at the d-meter. The readings were still climbing. The closer you got to the centre of Teijouan, and the Rift, the worse the effects were. The d-field didn't just mess with electronics – it screwed with your head. Get too deep into it for too long, you risked losing your mind.

The sky flickered, changing from blue to darkest night and back again. Dutch glimpsed unfamiliar constellations scattered across a desolate sky, as sure a sign as any that the Rift had just birthed a new monster.

'Blockage up ahead,' said Nat. 'The next –'

'The next turnoff on the right,' she said, slowing the car. 'I've been here before, remember?'

Nat pursed his lips and said nothing.

A pile of crumbling wreckage had blocked this section of coast road for as long as the Devil's Run had existed, but a well-mapped detour cut through the ruins of a nearby village. She drove past a cluster of bleached white bones the size of girders, and a kaiju skull twice as big as the Coupé.

The smoke billowed upwards from the other side of the village.

'D-meter's still climbing,' warned Nat. 'This detour takes us deeper into the d-field. We could wait it out…'

'No. Could be days before it drops again.'

She drove between ruined and empty buildings, headed north-east – deeper into the derangement field. The air throbbed like something alive and she wondered when she'd start seeing things.

'Next left,' said Nat. 'Then left again, and we're headed back west.'

Dutch nodded, tantalising shapes dancing at the edge of her vision like a promise of incipient madness. The next turn took them into a street lined with mismatched buildings, the road potholed and uneven. Halfway down, she saw that the smoke rose in a tall black column from a Toyota Hilux knocked over on its side.

General Hurley's car, she remembered, her heart bouncing around inside her chest like a frightened starling. She saw a pair of blackened outlines inside the blazing wreck.

'Could be whatever killed them is still around,' said Nat.

'Won't know for sure until it shows itself,' said Dutch. 'Take a picture while you can.'

Nat nodded, digging around beneath the dashboard before producing an old-style Polaroid camera. Normally they'd retrieve the film canisters too and collect the bounty for whatever footage they contained, but those had gone up in flames with the Hilux.

Nat pointed the camera out the window and took a snap of the Hilux as Dutch pulled up alongside. The camera whirred and spat out a square piece of paper. Nat peeled off the backing and waved the photograph in the air to help it dry.

'We've hardly started and that's one team down already.' He shook his head. 'That's got to be a bad omen.'

'I liked Hurley,' said Dutch. 'If it'd been Elektron or even the Countess, I wouldn't feel so bad.'

While she talked, Nat got a pen from the glove compartment and scrawled the time on the back of the picture. Then he pulled one of the rocket launchers free of a rear rack. He aimed it out the open window and nodded to Dutch. 'Figured we'd best not take any chances.'

'In my experience, Nat, the most you'll do is annoy the hell out of whatever killed Hurley with that thing.' She got them moving forward again. 'That's why I only ever use weapons as a last resort. You've got a far better chance of outrunning a kaiju than taking it down.'

They got back to the coast road without further incident, and the d-field loosened its grip on them. The hills on the inland side grew higher and more primordial. Just when Dutch thought they'd left any trouble behind them, a sudden, powerful tremor almost caused her to lose control of the Coupé. She looked up and saw something the size of a blockade ship come crashing down the hillside towards them, roaring like a chainsaw with laryngitis.

A blackjack, Dutch realised with horror; one of the ugliest, biggest and meanest types of kaiju. But also, as she knew from experience, painfully dim.

Dutch pressed the gas pedal down as far as it would go, hoping to outrun the beast before it reached the road. Nat, meanwhile, struggled to get his rocket launcher aimed at the beast.

'Nat!' Dutch yelled. 'Don't –'

Too late: a missile went corkscrewing through the air like an oversized firework, striking the slope a dozen metres above the descending Blackjack.

'If you're going to shoot at all, at least shoot *at* the damn kaiju, you asshole!'

But then she saw the missile had triggered a mini-avalanche, rocks and boulders tumbling down from higher up the slope and striking the Blackjack on its head and shoulders with sufficient force that it, too, went tumbling. It crashed to a halt before it even reached the coast highway.

'Not bad, right?' said Nat as they passed the kaiju by.

'I could still have outrun it,' she said. 'All you've done is piss it off.'

He stared at her with a look of incredulity. The Coupé's tyres screeched as they took the next bend, and the next.

'You can slow down,' he said. 'It won't come after us.'

'We're in a *race*, Nat. The whole *point* is to drive fast.'

'We're not here to win –'

'Maybe it's about time you told me what the fuck we *are* here for,' she shot back.

He pushed the rocket launcher into the back. 'Fine,' he said. 'We're going inland.'

At first she thought she'd misheard him. 'Say again?'

'I said, we're –'

She turned her attention back to the road in time to see the same Blackjack reappear on their right, smashing through small houses and sending trees tumbling before it landed on the motorway before them, its jaws wide.

'Brake!' Nat screamed.

Dutch did nothing of the kind. Instead she took a left that sent them hurtling through bushes before landing on the shore. The car bounced and shook as she pushed it forward, driving through another cluster of bushes and back onto the coast road. The kaiju, meanwhile, lumbered through a half-circle as it tried to track them.

'Check the map!' she screamed. 'I think there's a road tunnel up ahead.'

Nat twisted the paper around until he had it oriented the right way. 'There is, about half a kilometre ahead.'

The road continued to bend and twist as it followed the contours of the land. Then she saw it, dead ahead – a tunnel that drilled straight through the hillside. She made for it at speed, all too aware that any mistake would be her last. Once they were inside the tunnel, she pulled over, listening to the beast as it bellowed in impotent rage.

They sat like that for a minute without speaking. 'A word of advice, Nat,' she said at last. 'Don't shoot the damn things unless you have to. It's counter-productive, believe me.'

'Fair enough,' said Nat, his voice small and still.

She pushed the door open. 'I need to stretch my legs.'

She got out and walked towards the tunnel exit. The ground still trembled as the kaiju thudded about somewhere outside. After another minute, Nat came to join her.

*How long has it been*? She wondered. *An hour into the race? And as close as I've ever come to dying.*

In that moment, Dutch realised her five years in jail were the reason she was still alive.

'You said we were going inland.'

'That's right.'

She let out a slow breath. 'Nobody's gone inland and returned with their sanity intact since before they evacuated Teijouan. It's impossible.'

'But say a shortcut existed,' he said. 'A place where the

derangement field doesn't affect you. A safe corridor, stretching the whole way across the island from one coast to the other.'

She turned to stare at him. 'Bullshit.'

'Someone did it – got to the Rift and back and lived to talk about it.'

'What happened to them?'

Nat shrugged. 'They died. Eventually.'

Dutch felt a tightness in her chest like she was about to have a heart attack, and realised she was holding her breath. 'Not what I'd call encouraging.'

Nat stepped closer to the tunnel exit and listened. 'I can't hear it. Maybe it's gone.'

Dutch didn't share his optimism, but then again they couldn't hide in the tunnel forever. Nat followed her back over to the Coupé and slid in beside her.

'I want you to tell me everything,' she said, one hand on the wheel, 'starting the moment we're sure the coast is clear.'

'Sure. Nice driving back there, by the way.'

She regarded him coolly for a moment, and started the engine.

Dutch eased the Coupé out of the tunnel at a bare crawl, peering up the neighbouring slope, ready to reverse back inside at a moment's notice. She took it slow at first, afraid of drawing the Blackjack to them with the noise of the engine, but they saw no further sign of it. Before long, they reached the outskirts of Takau.

Dutch checked the dashboard and observed that the day was heading towards evening. 'Tell me the rest.'

'Back about nine years ago, they rescued someone alive from the ruins of a coastal village near Truku Gorge. He'd been there for years, since before the Rift first formed. The way he babbled at the ship's crew who found him, they figured constant exposure to the d-field had fried his brain. They put him in an asylum and forgot about him until he died a few months back.'

'And?'

'The coroner who autopsied him found a map, tattooed onto his chest. It showed a route cutting across the centre of the island, starting from Shinchiku in the north-west and cutting across to Truku Gorge in the East, passing a few kilometres north of the Rift. Apparently, during his more lucid moments while he was still alive, the man was in the habit of insisting he'd found a safe route across the island.'

'And nobody believed him?'

'Would you have?'

Dutch's hands flexed on the wheel. A shortcut – impossible as it seemed – would cut most of a day out of the race. She pictured herself breaking the all-time round-island record and felt a rush of adrenaline. 'Go on.'

'Wu learned of it and locked the coroner into a very expensive NDA. Six weeks ago, he had a remote-controlled robot sent along the same route as the map on the dead guy's chest. The robot got most of the way to the Rift without its electronics losing any of their functionality – which is, I'm sure you'll agree, unprecedented. So Wu had his people follow up with a manned scientific expedition aboard an armoured RV.'

'I never heard about any of this.'

'With good reason,' said Nat. 'Anyway, the RV and everyone on board disappeared without trace. We figured kaiju got them all, but then a week ago a survivor made his way to the coast on foot and fired off a distress flare. A Japanese corvette picked him up. He'd been burned by kaiju venom and died within a day. But first, he gave this to his rescuers.'

Nat reached inside his driving suit and pulled out a thin, cigarette-length rod of dull grey metal. He passed it over and Dutch took a hand from the wheel to study it, turning it this way and that.

'Doesn't look like something worth dying for,' she said

dismissively, passing it back.

'It's worth a thousand times its weight in gold or diamonds. This,' Nat explained, 'is a room-temperature superconductor.'

'A what?'

'The solution to all the world's energy problems, Dutch. Before he died, the scientist who brought it back insisted there were a lot more where this came from.'

'So what killed the rest of the expedition? Kaiju?'

Nat shrugged. 'That's the assumption.'

'Who did they take with them?'

He shook his head. 'I don't understand.'

'A driver,' she said. 'Someone experienced with kaiju. You're not going to tell me Wu sent those people inland without any kind of backup?'

When Nat didn't answer, she looked at him.

'Jesus,' she said. 'You're kidding me.'

'There was a concern that if they involved someone from outside, even an experienced driver, word might get out of what they'd found. They went in on their own.'

She laughed bitterly. 'Dumb fucking mistake.'

'That's why you're here, Dutch. So we don't make the same mistake twice.'

'So why all the subterfuge? Why break me out of jail, instead of sending in another expedition?'

'Word got out about what we'd found, and Wu's afraid Strugatsky might try to grab the rest of the rods first. That means we have to be sneaky to avoid triggering him into a pre-emptive grab.'

'You said the route starts near Shinchiku. Where, exactly?'

'I'll tell you when we get there.'

'What do you think I'll do, shoot you and steal the map?'

He favoured her with a thin smile. 'I'd rather not find out.'

*Thanks a bunch, asshole*. 'And after we find the rest of these super-whatsit rods? What then?'

'We hide out for a while. Then we follow the route to the East Coast, and drive south to the finishing line.'

She frowned. 'Why hide out?'

'Because if we get back to the Security Zone in half the time it takes anyone else, it'll be pretty obvious we found a shortcut. If we wait before rejoining the race, we'll get there about the same time as the other teams.'

She felt a tingling in her skin. 'But we *could* come first. We could –'

'No,' he said, his voice flat. 'You've never come first in the Devil's Run, Dutch – not once. We're not taking any chances that might arouse suspicion.'

A sour sensation pooled in her belly. 'Because we're not here to win the race,' she muttered, imitating his Australian accent.

He glared at her. 'Correct.'

Her hands gripped the steering wheel hard enough to hurt. 'Sun's coming down,' she said, her voice tight with fury. Driving after nightfall was too much of a risk since headlamps drew kaiju to them like sharks to a surfer. 'We should look for someplace safe for the night.'

They soon left the ruins of Takau behind them. Ahead lay Shinchiku, a hundred and fifty kilometres further up the coast. The first evening stars came out as she drove.

Dutch found she wanted to believe Nat, no matter how the rational part of her mind insisted a cross-island route was impossible. There had been rumours, but even if such a thing had existed, nobody was suicidal or foolhardy enough to go searching for it. For a long time it had been little more than a myth, something which couldn't be real.

But if such a route *did* exist, whoever successfully navigated it would become an instant legend – assuming they could ever talk about it: and the idea she might not made Dutch want to scream. She knew she'd done a less than stellar job of hiding her frustration from the way Nat cast occasional worried glances at her.

They came to another stretch of coast road that had crumbled away, and so turned inland, following a suggested detour that led them to the remains of a small town. The d-meter flickered, showing low readings. Before long Dutch threaded the Coupé through narrow streets half-blocked by debris. At one point, they got out and pushed the Coupé most of a kilometre after spotting the hulking outline of a Silverback sleeping amidst the ruins.

They were still looking for a place to hide until daybreak when they heard the dull roar of an engine, a few kilometres north of their position. Dutch guessed they weren't the only ones trying to find somewhere safe to spend the night.

They decided at last to park the Coupé inside the foyer of a hotel. Nat took care of storing the film they'd taken so far in the boot, putting new film into the cameras mounted front and rear.

Most of the upper floors had collapsed, making them inaccessible, so they crossed the road and broke into the stockroom of a neighbouring 7/11. The moon had risen, flickering as its light passed through the d-field. Even though the readings stayed low, Dutch still saw furtive shapes moving at the edges of her vision. She didn't like being this deep in the d-field, but they had little choice.

She spread a sleeping bag on top of some flattened cardboard boxes in the stockroom. Nat took first watch sitting on the shop's counter, a rifle by his side. She flicked through a few pages of a discarded manga by torch-light, wondering what the words said, then fell asleep almost without realising it.

Dutch came awake a short while before dawn to steady, rhythmic vibrations rolling through the ground beneath her. She rolled upright, listening until they faded. The sleeping Silverback they'd skirted earlier must have risen from its slumber.

Stepping out of the stockroom, she found Nat asleep with his back against the counter, the rifle propped by his side. Even a passing kaiju wasn't enough to wake him.

The moon didn't flicker when she slipped outside and looked up at the night sky. She made her way across the road and inside the hotel foyer, her feet crunching on broken glass.

Nat had stashed the navigator's map in the glove compartment, along with a second torch. She found her old bandana in there as well, and she pocketed it before spreading the map on her knees. She had to risk turning on the torch so she could see it. She saw that he had marked the safe route with a thick black diagonal line slashing across the map, starting from north of Shinchiku and following a series of twisting roads through Teijouan's central mountains to the East.

Something clattered outside the hotel, and Dutch froze, hearing scuffling movement. She switched off the torch.

She waited, lungs tight in her chest, and heard nothing more. Even so, she reached into the back of the car and took hold of a rifle. She sank low in the seat with the rifle gripped in both hands, the map discarded beside her.

'Help me,' cried a man's voice, ragged and full of terror.

Dutch listened to the sound of her own breathing for a long moment, then pushed herself back upright, her throat tight with terror. Whoever the stranger might be, it sounded like they were right outside.

'Please,' said the voice, sounding weaker now. 'For God's sake. Help me!'

The rifle felt warm in her grasp.

'Please!'

She pushed the Coupé's door open as silently as possible and slid out, keeping low. She moved with careful steps towards the foyer entrance, ready to duck back into the shadows.

Could be it was another driver, injured after a kaiju attack.

She couldn't deny there was something deeply familiar about the voice.

Then she remembered why.

She came to a halt. It wasn't possible, and yet she'd recognise that voice anywhere. And as Nat himself had said, sometimes people found a way to survive on Teijouan, sometimes for years…

She swallowed hard and moved out into the street. Then she saw him: Johnny Lear, crouched low by the entrance to an alley, one leg soaked in blood. He was breathing with difficulty, his face drained of colour.

'Dutch,' he said, his voice ragged. 'I can't believe it's you.'

She stared at him. 'You can't be here.' *Or alive.*

'I'm hurt.' He reached a hand towards her. 'I need your help, Dutch –'

She heard a *click* from behind her, and in the next moment the side of Johnny's head exploded.

The air reverberated with the gunshot. She whirled around to see Nat standing outside the 7/11, his rifle still raised to his shoulder.

'What the *fuck* did you do!' she screamed.

'For Christ's sake, Dutch,' he yelled. 'Run!'

She turned back and saw something huge and reptilian crouching where Johnny had been. It dug long claws into the brick wall beside it and let out a shriek of pain and anger, the side of its long, cruel-looking snout dark with blood.

Nat fired a second shot, and then a third, and the creature – tiny by kaiju standards, being not much larger than an elephant – slid to the ground and became motionless.

Dutch stared at it, her blood cold and sluggish. 'What *is* that thing?'

Nat hurried over to her. 'A shapeshifter-kaiju.'

'I never heard of such a thing.'

'I guess you were in jail when the first ones appeared. What did you see?'

She turned to look at him. 'Johnny Lear.'

'I have no idea who that is,' said Nat, 'but what I saw looked like my sister, and she's been dead fifteen years.'

'Johnny was my first navigator.'

He grabbed her by the arm and pulled her back inside the foyer. 'It's about dawn. We should get moving in case the shots drew something else's attention.'

'But how did that thing *know*?'

'All anybody knows is somehow they can dig around inside your brain and show you the people or things you most care about. From that moment, unless you've got any idea what you're dealing with, you're dead meat.'

'You're telling me they can *read minds*?'

'It's no crazier than anything else on this damn island,' he pointed out. He started to get inside the Coupé and shot her an accusing look. 'You were looking at the map.'

*Shit.* 'So?'

He stared at her. 'I hope you weren't thinking of driving off and leaving me here.'

She glared at him. 'I wanted to see where we were going, is all.'

He swore under his breath and tossed his rifle in the back. 'Lucky for you the only thing I care about is getting the hell out of here before something else comes sniffing around.'

# SIDEKICK DU JOUR

The morning proved to be cool and foggy, with mist clinging close to the ground, and Dutch struggled to see further than a few hundred metres in the dawn light. She drove at a slow crawl, but before long the day got brighter and the road ascended, lifting them above the fog. She glanced to the East, seeing tall mountains towards the centre of Teijouan. The cameras recorded it all.

They came to a halt, seeing the road bridge ahead of them had collapsed into a gorge. 'That was still standing last time I came this way,' she said.

'Looks like it fell down sometime after last year's race,' said Nat, looking over the map. 'We'll just figure out another route.'

Dutch pushed the door open and got out. Nat kept poring over the map, trying to find a way across or around the gorge. She shielded her eyes with one hand and peered north. Shinchiku's skyline was about visible, far off on the horizon.

As she watched, a tiny orange star rose from amidst the ruins.

'Hey!' She turned and shouted to Nat. 'Look.'

He got out and joined her. The flare ascended further, then faded. 'That's the Countess' signal.'

Dutch nodded. 'She's reached the first rendezvous. We need to move faster.'

'Once again, we are *not* here to –'

'I heard you the first time,' she snapped. 'But we still need to refuel before we make the crossing.'

Nat spread the map on top of the Coupé's roof. 'Take a look,' he said, beckoning her over. 'There's a river down in that gorge. The map says it's shallow enough, I think it might be possible for us to drive straight across it.'

'But how do we even get down there?'

His fingers traced a route on the paper. 'A switchback road leads to the bottom of the gorge and back up the other side. It'll take time, but any other route takes us too far inland.'

Dutch sucked her teeth. 'Risky, though. Someone like Vishnevsky can ford a river in that tank of his, but the Coupé's a different matter.'

'We might as well check it out. We'd be crazy not to.'

She agreed to his proposal with some reluctance. They took a road off the highway and navigated their way down the switchback road. The road veered back and forth down the slope of the gorge like a madman's scribble, but they were soon driving past warehouses and shops lining the banks of the river.

Nat turned out to be right; the water only covered their ankles. 'It's been a dry season,' he noted. 'No way we'd be able to get across if there'd been rain any time in the last few weeks.'

Dutch used a low gear, easing the Coupé across the shallow flow. Another road ascended the opposite slope with yet more switchbacks, its flanks covered in what appeared at first to be tiny houses. Closer investigation revealed it to be a cemetery, the houses mausoleums.

They were approaching the top of the hill when Doktor Elektron's Peterbilt semi came roaring out from behind the cover of an electrical substation, catching the rear of the Coupé and spinning it halfway around in a circle. The impact slammed Dutch's head against the wheel and she tasted blood. Her vision swam, but she stayed conscious. Beside her, Nat groaned and swallowed with apparent difficulty.

She looked out the window and saw Elektron reversing his truck. If he rammed them a second time, they were dead.

Dutch reached for the ignition and tried to start the engine again; it coughed once, then fell silent.

She tried again: still nothing.

Ice coated the inside of her chest as she stared at the key. She considered getting out of the car and running.

Third time lucky, she told herself, and tried again.

This time it caught.

The tyres bit into the tarmac with a screech. The Coupé lurched forward and out of the way barely in time. She caught a glimpse in the mirror of Elektron slamming on the brakes before he plunged through the road-barrier and down into the gorge. He reversed and spun the wheel to pursue them, Kid Atomik by his side.

The Coupé, by some miracle, remained functional. They picked up speed, steering past several ancient wrecks. The road still climbed ahead of them; one last switchback, then they were back on level ground.

She almost shouted in triumph when she saw Elektron slipping to the rear. Then the Coupé inexplicably started to slow down, like one of those nightmares where you stay rooted to the spot no matter how fast you run.

'What's wrong with it?' she screamed.

'Dutch,' croaked Nat. 'The engine.'

Steam came pouring out of the hood and Dutch worked the

gas pedal to no effect. The car rolled past several more wrecks before drifting to a halt. She pounded the dashboard with a fist, screaming her frustration.

'Out,' yelled Nat, pushing his door open and disappearing from view.

Dutch at least had the foresight to put on the brake before getting out and running. They were at the uppermost edge of the graveyard, and she saw a small mausoleum like a stone hut in pink and grey stone behind a low concrete wall. She made towards it, seeking cover.

Shots cracked through the air as she threw herself flat behind the wall. She crouched low, bullets gouging chunks of stone from out of the mausoleum's walls.

The shooting stopped. She listened, hearing voices, although not well enough to make out what they were saying. One she recognised as Doktor Elektron, while the other had to be Kid Atomik, his sidekick *du jour*.

A gap in the wall allowed access to a short concrete path that led into the interior of the mausoleum. Dutch belly-crawled over to the gap and peered out: Elektron's truck had pulled to a halt twenty metres further down the road. Past the opposite verge lay nothing but a sheer drop.

She watched as Kid Atomik climbed onto the roof of the semi's cabin. He lay flat, studying the road through a rifle fitted with a telescopic sight.

The rifle twitched towards Dutch and she ducked back. A bullet knocked another chunk out of the wall behind her. The Coupé wasn't hard to spot, given the steam still pouring from under its hood.

'Hey, Atomik!' she yelled, her voice echoing in the still, flat air.

'What?'

'You've got a stupid fucking name, you know that?'

'Yeah?' His voice sounded high and reedy. 'Whatever the

fuck kind of a girl's name is Dutch?'

Another shot knocked chunks out of the mausoleum. She glanced back out through the gap, wondering where in hell Nat had got to.

Assuming Elektron or the kid hadn't killed him.

Now she had time to think, it was clear Elektron had planned his ambush well. He'd known the collapsed bridge would most likely force them to drive across the river and take the road up the side of the gorge. All he'd had to do was sit up here and wait.

'You might as well come out from hiding,' shouted Elektron. She couldn't see him, but he sounded close. 'Your car looks trashed.'

'How about you give us your truck instead?' Dutch yelled.

Elektron laughed wheezily. 'Where's your boyfriend?'

'No idea, but I can see yours on top of that truck.'

'This isn't a fucking joke, McGuire!'

'You dumb shit,' she bellowed, 'I'll bet your dick hasn't been this hard in years.'

She risked another glance and spotted Nat, still alive and crouched behind a hatchback. He nodded to her and put a finger to his lips.

Elektron darted out from cover, a Beretta machine pistol gripped in both hands. He ran behind another wreck before dropping out of sight. Dutch swore under her breath. Neither of them had thought to grab a weapon before they abandoned the Coupé. But from the way Elektron kept running from cover to cover, he didn't know that.

'How much did Muto pay you?' shouted Dutch.

'I want to talk to your navigator,' Elektron shouted back. 'I know what he stole from Strugatsky!'

She looked over at Nat and mouthed *what the hell?* But Nat shook his head.

A shadow passed over the mausoleum building. Dutch

craned her head back and saw something huge and winged pass low over the gorge. A second later a terrified shriek echoed up and down the road, followed by the sound of rapid gunfire.

She ducked her head back out. Elektron stood out in the open, his back to both her and Nat. He'd lifted his Beretta to fire up at an enormous winged kaiju flying into the distance, Kid Atomik wriggling in its massive claws.

Nat didn't waste time, jumping up from his hiding-place and charging Elektron, knocking him flat. The Beretta went skittering across the road, and Nat rolled Elektron onto his back, flailing at him with his fists until he stopped struggling. Dutch meanwhile ran over and snatched up the Beretta before training it on Elektron.

'Shit.' Nat jumped back up, alarm on his face. Elektron stayed put, his face bloodied and bruised. 'I forgot about those damn gloves of his.'

'Uh-uh,' said Dutch. 'His suit won't work here, remember?'

Nat's eyes widened. 'Good point.' He pressed one boot on Elektron's neck. 'You hear that, dickface?'

Elektron's eyes rolled in his head and he gurgled something inaudible. Dutch scanned the sky; she had a feeling the kaiju wouldn't return until after it had eaten its lunch. Nat yanked down the zip on the front of Elektron's driving suit and rummaged around inside before pulling out a familiar red envelope.

Dutch snatched it from him and pulled out a sheet of rice-paper covered in Japanese calligraphy. 'So you *were* working for Muto,' said Nat, staring at Elektron with contempt.

Elektron stared back up at him with an angry scowl, his skin damp with sweat and the B.O. coming off him in waves. 'That's only part of it, and you damn well know why.'

'What did you mean when you said Nat stole something from Strugatsky?' asked Dutch.

Elektron looked between them in confusion, his domino

mask askew, then. 'You're serious? You don't know?'

'Nope.'

A faltering grin caught one side of his mouth and he looked back at Nat. 'How about it, navigator? You gonna tell her the truth?'

Dutch fired the Beretta into the road a few inches from Elektron's head. He jerked back and regarded her with silent horror.

'Cut the bullshit,' she roared. '*What* did he steal?'

Elektron's gaze shifted between them. 'A map.'

*You piece of shit, Nat.* 'One that leads past the Rift?'

Elektron nodded frantically.

Blood pulsed in her head as she turned to look at Nat. 'Is this true?'

Nat shook his head in disgust, then turned and walked a few feet away.

A greasy smile spread across Elektron's face. 'Shit, he really kept you in the dark, didn't he?'

'There was an expedition,' said Dutch. 'I know that much.'

Elektron nodded. 'Strugatsky sent a bunch of his scientists here to find what they could, except most of them disappeared.'

Dutch twitched the barrel of the Beretta towards Nat, who had turned back to regard them both. 'I asked you if what he's saying is true.'

Nat's eyes grew larger. 'Dutch –'

She steadied her aim, Elektron forgotten for the moment. '*Tell me.*'

'Fine,' he said. 'Strugatsky sent in the expedition, not Wu.'

'Strugatsky knew someone had hacked into his secure networks and stolen data related to the map, along with samples of the superconductors, so he hired Muto to find out who,' Elektron told her, pushing himself up onto his elbows. 'Once he realised Wu had put you in the race, Dutch, he figured you were being sent here to retrieve the rest of them from under his nose.'

Dutch took a step back so she could train the Beretta on both of them. 'That still doesn't explain why you had one of Madame Muto's death notices in your jacket.'

'Listen,' said Elektron, licking thin, greasy lips, 'you've got the advantage here, and that's cool. We've been friends a long time, and –'

She fired another shot into the tarmac near Elektron's head and he scrabbled backwards, closer to Nat. 'Okay, okay!' he said in a panic. 'Muto came to me with an offer two days before the race.'

*Two days*? That meant Muto had discovered she'd be in the Devil's Run after Wu decided to put her in it, but before he broke her out of jail. Hiro would have done most of the work of digging up the information for her.

'To do what?' Dutch asked. 'Stop us getting to the superconductors first, or to kill me?'

'…kind of both.'

Something still didn't add up, though she couldn't quite place her finger on it. 'And this was on Strugatksy's orders?'

'Maybe Muto used your vendetta with her to cover up the real reason she wanted you dead – because Strugatsky paid her to have you killed and keep us out of the race.'

Dutch had to admit it made sense, but something still niggled at her.

She moved closer to Elektron, poking him in the chest with the Beretta. 'How did you manage to cut the fuel line in the Coupé?'

Elektron stared at her in utter confusion. 'What?'

She poked the barrel hard against his chest. 'Stop bullshitting me. How did you do it?'

'For the love of God, Dutch, I swear I don't know what you're talking about!'

'Why should I believe you, when you were sneaking around our car before the time-trials?'

'Okay, fine,' Elektron admitted. 'I meant to plant a tracker – something real simple that'd work as long as you didn't go too deep into the d-field. But you found me before I had a chance to do so. But I don't know anything about a fuel line!'

'Of course he cut it,' said Nat. 'I don't think one true word's ever come out of his mouth.'

It occurred to Dutch that if Elektron *had* cut their fuel line, it would have been with the intention of doubling back and murdering them while they were stranded in the middle of nowhere.

Instead, he'd waited until now. Which meant he might be telling the truth, and somebody else had cut the line… which meant, in turn, that somebody else in the race was out to kill her.

She pinched the skin between her eyes and massaged it. 'I need to think about this.'

'Dutch,' Elektron said in a half-whisper, low enough Nat wouldn't hear him. 'You don't need that guy – he's been lying to you the whole time. But if you and me team up maybe we –'

Dutch shot Elektron in the thigh. He let out a full-blooded scream that rapidly dissolved into animal-like whimpering, his face bloodless and quivering.

Dutch swung the Beretta back towards Nat. 'He's got one thing right – you lied to me.'

'I had no part in that decision,' he said. 'For what it's worth, I didn't agree with it. But I had my orders from Wu.'

Dutch felt her face twist into a snarl. 'I swear to God I should leave the pair of you assholes here to rot.'

'We got you out of jail,' Nat pointed out. 'If you turn up at that finishing line without me and Wu even suspects you abandoned me, he'll throw you straight back in that Russian cesspit, and you know it.'

'And if I talked?'

'There are easier ways to commit suicide.'

'Listen to me, Dutch,' said Elektron, his face stiff with pain.

'He's still keeping things back from you, like what the Rift actually *is*.'

'Are you going to listen to any more of this bullshit?' asked Nat.

'Shut up,' said Dutch. She nodded to Elektron. 'How about *you* tell me?'

'It's the one question everybody wants the answer to,' said Elektron, biting the words out. 'See, back when the Rift first formed, everyone got to running around in a panic thinking the North Koreans had nuked Teijouan. Except then the first kaiju appeared, and they realised something else had happened.'

'You're not telling me anything I don't already know.'

'Yeah, but then a rumour went around that maybe the Americans had been developing some kind of weapon in league with the Teijouan authorities.'

'I've heard that bullshit rumour before,' she said. 'Don't try to test me.'

'No, Dutch, it's true. Except it wasn't a weapon – it was an experiment. See, they built a secret facility up in the mountains where they could use death-row prisoners as guinea pigs. Wired them up to computers and fed them full of drugs.' A peculiar fervour came into Elektron's voice. 'They were trying to hack the underlying code that controls reality itself, but they did it too well. They opened a door they couldn't close.'

'Where did you get this crap from?' she demanded.

'Wu knows the truth,' Elektron insisted, jerking his chin towards Nat. 'So does Strugatsky. That's why they don't let anyone but us onto the island, not even scientists, except for their own people – it's all a cover-up.'

'You're saying they had something to do with it?' Dutch demanded, curious now despite herself. 'Strugatsky and Wu?'

'Sure,' said Elektron, his voice stiff with pain. 'The two of them were partners once, everybody knows that. They had the contract to run the experimental program back when they were still partners. I saw it all, along with the data about the map.' He stared wild-eyed at Nat. 'He'll confirm it all. Just ask him!'

'You said something about a door,' said Dutch.

'Not like a regular door,' said Elektron. 'The Rift is more like a… a singularity, a point where different parallel realities merge. Like a crossroads, except it doesn't have four paths – it has millions.' The crazed gleam in his eyes intensified. 'The kaiju come through that door from some other place. But we can go through the other way, Dutch. And not just to where the kaiju come from – to anywhere we want.'

She shook her head, feeling something almost akin to admiration. 'You must be one crazy motherfucker to come up with a story like that, Elektron.'

'Listen to me!' Elektron rasped. *'Ask Nat.* He knows!'

'Sounds like the d-field fried his brain,' suggested Nat.

'Why would Nat want to keep all this back from me, even assuming one dumbass word of it isn't some random shit you made up?' she asked Elektron.

'Because the d-field is getting bigger. The blockade's been measuring its fluctuations for years, and before long it'll spread beyond the island. Ten, twenty, a hundred years from now it could end up swallowing the whole damn world.'

'Let's pretend I believe one word of this,' said Dutch. 'Then how could anyone know there's a way through the Rift without actually going through it?'

'Some of those scientists Strugatsky sent survived long enough to do exactly that – crossed over, then came back to tell what they'd found. Then they went back through for good.'

'He knows the more you let him talk, the longer he lives,' said Nat. 'We're wasting time.'

'Take me with you,' Elektron pleaded, all but ignoring Nat now. 'You'll see it's true. I'll go through the Rift and never come back, I swear. That's been my plan all along – I could give a rat's ass about Muto or the money!'

'You're not going anywhere,' said Dutch, slugging Elektron in the head with the butt of the gun. He slumped back against the crash-barrier, his eyes rolling up in his skull. Dutch crumpled up the death notice and threw it down beside him.

'We should check the Coupé,' said Nat. 'See if she still runs.'

Dutch pointed the Beretta at him. '*You* can stay where the hell you are until I decide whether you get to ride with me or not.'

He had the good sense not to say anything more as she stalked back over to the Coupé. The right rear panel was crushed, and the window on that same side cracked and starred. The tyres still looked good, though. She raised the hood and looked inside.

It didn't take long for Dutch to work out that a coolant hose had cracked. Given how much worse things could have been, they'd been lucky – very, very lucky.

At first she thought she could trim off the cracked part of the hose and stretch what remained to fit the gasket. It quickly became clear that wasn't going to work. She went hunting through some of the nearby wrecks until she found one that fit. Soon she had everything back in place and checked the engine by letting it run for a while. The Coupé looked like she'd been through a war, but as long as the engine ran, little else mattered.

'We're going,' she announced over her shoulder, closing the hood.

Nat came over and stood by the passenger door as if waiting for permission. 'So are we…?'

'Get in,' she said. 'But don't expect me to trust you.'

'Right.' He glanced at Elektron, now stirring back to life. 'What about him?'

Dutch thought for a minute, took a single bullet and a pistol from one of the racks, and carried them over to Elektron's Peterbilt semi.

First, she stripped Elektron's ride of its used film canisters, carrying them over to the Coupé and dumping them in the boot with all the rest. Then she climbed inside the semi-truck's cabin, selecting a snub-nosed rifle from Elektron's weapons racks that turned out to be just about the right length to wedge the gas pedal flat against the floor. She turned on the ignition and jumped back down onto the road just as the truck started to roll forward.

By the time she'd picked herself back up, the truck had burst through the road-side crash barrier, sailing off down the side of the cliff. It made a lot of noise on the way down.

She turned to see Elektron balancing on his one good leg, staring at the space where his vehicle had been. 'You…' he seemed to be unable to find the right words. 'You… *fucking*…'

'Sorry, Doc,' she said, stepping closer to him and pushing the single bullet into his hand. 'Couldn't take a chance on you coming after us again.'

He stared down at the bullet. 'What the fuck is this for?'

Dutch threw the pistol back the way she'd come, and it slid to a halt a few metres short of the crash-barrier. 'One bullet, one gun. If you're lucky, you'll get to the next rendezvous on foot and be able to fire off a distress beacon. If you're not lucky, something'll eat you first.'

'What the hell do I do with one bullet?'

'Better than none.' She shrugged. 'Or you could shoot yourself. Either way, I don't care.'

She got back inside the Coupé and motioned for Nat to join her. She took one last glance at Elektron, still standing right where they'd left him, his face full of stricken horror. Right before they turned the next corner, she saw him limping over to where she'd thrown the pistol.

'Dutch –' Nat started to say.

'Shut up,' she said, her voice thick with fury. 'I've met some of the worst people in the world in jail, and right now I'd rather have their company than yours. So keep the fuck quiet and be glad you're not fighting over that bullet with that asshole.'

He pointed up. 'I only meant to say that kaiju is on the way back.'

Dutch pulled the Coupé over to one side, keeping them hidden beneath some overhanging trees. The kaiju's shadow swept over them and kept on going, headed back to where they'd been seconds before. Dutch heard a single shot, followed by a terrified shriek, and then silence.

# TO THE RIFT

They didn't talk for a while after that.

They reached the outskirts of Shinchiku, a medium-sized metropolis on Teijouan's North-West Coast as silent and empty as any other on the island. Nat kept himself busy with the maps, not looking up until they coasted to a halt midway down a broad avenue.

He looked up from his maps. 'Why'd you stop?'

'Up there.' Dutch pointed at the flat roof of a building that, according to a faded sign in English and Chinese, had been a bank. A car sat on the roof, its front wheels sticking out over the street below, as if something had picked it up and dropped it there. Which, she suspected, had in fact occurred.

'Looks familiar,' said Nat. 'Hard to be sure, without seeing more than the undercarriage…'

Dutch looked closer at the vehicle's armoured wheels. 'That's Lucifer Black's car,' she said suddenly.

'Holy…' Nat cracked his door open to get a better look.

'You're right,' he said, shading his eyes as he peered upwards.

Dutch snagged the Polaroid camera from under the dashboard and got out. She took a quick snap of the wreck, and waited for the picture to develop. 'We should go up there,' she said.

Nat climbed the rest of the way out of the car and squinted at her. 'Both of us?'

'This is the same asshole got you nearly trampled by Long Tall Sally,' she reminded him. *Not to mention there's no way in hell I'm letting you out of my sight.* 'Wouldn't you rather make sure the son of a bitch is dead?'

He stared back up at the wreck. 'Now that you put it that way…'

She smiled to herself as she followed him over.

The building had been knocked about hard enough that at first Dutch was far from sure they'd ever find a way up to the roof, but they struck lucky, finding a stairwell in the rear that was still intact. At the top they found a door held shut by an ancient and badly rusted padlock that shattered after Nat gave it three hard kicks, coming apart in a cloud of orange dust. They made their way outside onto the roof and saw Lucifer Black's vehicle sitting next to a concrete ventilation shaft, its rear wheels hanging out over the street below.

'I'm amazed it took this long for his luck to run out,' said Dutch. She thought for a moment. 'Or hers.'

Nat's eyes widened. 'You think there's a chance he's still alive in there?'

She gave him a look.

'Or her,' he said, rolling his eyes.

'I guess we're about to find out,' she said, handing him the Polaroid and stepping closer.

She cracked a door open and looked inside, careful not to put her weight on the car in case the pressure sent it sliding the rest of the way off the edge of the roof.

At first, Dutch couldn't make sense of anything inside Black's car. Instead of Dietrich Sokoloff or anyone else, all she could see was a dense tangle of goofy-looking electronics that filled almost the entirety of the stripped-out interior, most of it wrapped around a central mass about two metres in length and suspended in the centre of the car by dozens of steel cables. Black's car had no seats, nor could she see a dashboard.

Nat peered inside from just behind her shoulder. 'Damn – maybe they *did* run the thing by remote-control.'

Dutch laughed sourly. 'That's impossible, and you –' she stopped mid-sentence, staring at the twisted wires and circuitry.

'All right,' said Nat, stepping back again, 'not by remote-control, maybe. But there's nothing advanced in there – it's all tube valves and the like. The kind of primitive electronics that are the least likely to be affected by the d-field.'

She saw that he was right. 'You'd have to stick close to the periphery, though,' she noted. The more she looked at the elongated bundle suspended by wires, the more it resolved into something else…

*A suit.* Now that she could see it, under the dense tangle of wires and tubes, it was obvious. The suit contained a person. Sokoloff?

Or someone else?

She reached in past a tangle of wires and primitive circuitry and touched the suit. Judging by the smell alone, whoever – or whatever – was inside it was very dead. The face lay behind a mask with tubes protruding from the mouth and nose. She gingerly peeled back a layer of dark cloth near the neck and saw mottled, pale flesh with wires embedded into it. A layer of stubble identified Black's gender, but it was the wrong colour to be Sokoloff.

She stepped back from the car, feeling sick. 'He's a cyborg or something.'

'A what?'

'Part machine, part human,' she told Nat. 'Black isn't the car's driver – he *is* the car. That's why no one ever saw him, except maybe Sokoloff or whoever… built him.'

Nat shook his head. 'Damnedest thing.' He took a step back and started taking pictures with the Polaroid, while Dutch carefully retrieved the film from Black's rear-mounted camera.

They left Shinchiku behind and soon reached the first rendezvous point, next to a sewage plant. The other surviving racers had untangled the crates from their parachutes and left them with only slim pickings. Dutch tried not to think how far ahead they must be by now.

They topped up the Coupé's engine and loaded spare canisters of gas and water into the boot. Then Dutch dug out their flare gun and sent a green star shooting high into the air so the world would know they'd reached the first checkpoint.

Using a flare gun on Teijouan, however, carried its own special risks.

They'd got the engine started when a demented roar rolled across the landscape surrounding the sewage plant. They took off with a shriek and got moving fast before whatever they'd heard came after them.

'How long before we turn inland?' asked Dutch.

'The second turnoff ahead. It leads to a village fifty kilometres inland from here.'

Fifty kilometres: further into the d-field than anyone had ever been before. Or almost anyone, Dutch reminded herself.

They sped past a petrochemical complex and towards a forest spread across sloping terrain. Something huge moved through the trees at about two o'clock.

Moving to intercept them.

A Screecher burst out of the trees and into the middle of the highway, its multiple heads twisting on long, snakelike necks attached to a stumpy four-legged body. Dutch knew from experience that the creatures were half-blind in daylight, but they more than made up for it with their hearing. The Screecher's heads twisted around as it tried to zero in on their location by the sound of their engine.

'It's between us and that turnoff,' Dutch shouted.

'Take the next right,' said Nat. 'I think I can plot another detour.'

She swung the wheel, the car skidding and bouncing on the uneven road surface, and they passed between low, rusty shacks that soon gave way to the remains of a small settlement, the road cracked and overgrown with weeds.

The Screecher came lumbering after them, howling its anger. She glanced in a mirror in time to see one side of an apartment block collapse into dust and rubble as the kaiju crashed straight through it.

'Second left,' said Nat. 'That'll get us back to where we were going.'

The road opened up, the shacks replaced by tall office and residential buildings; they were back in Shinjuku's northernmost suburbs. Before Dutch could make the turn, one of the biggest Viper-Tails she'd ever seen in her life came careering around a corner up ahead and straight towards them, probably attracted by all the noise. It reared up on its hind legs, its head level with a neighbouring office block.

Dutch slammed the Coupé to a halt. 'Nat, I think we're –'

*Trapped,* she'd meant to say: but as she spoke, she caught sight of a shopping mall occupying the ground floor of the building to their immediate left. She could just about make out daylight on the other side of the building through its shattered façade. She twisted the wheel, then drove the Coupé up a set of concrete steps and into the interior of the mall.

The ground shook beneath their wheels as the two kaiju came thundering towards each other, the two humans and their car forgotten.

Dutch blasted past display units, steering almost by instinct in the dim half-light of the mall's interior. 'There!' shouted Nat, pointing forward as they passed beneath a tall, glass-roofed atrium. 'Ten o'clock!'

Dutch steered towards the rectangle of light and the Coupé went thumping down more steps and onto an empty and open road. Behind them, the kaiju fell to battle, shrieking their fury as they fought for domination.

*That's it*, thought Dutch. *After this, I'm retiring, whatever the hell else happens.*

They found their way to the turnoff and Dutch drove ten kilometres east before she pulled over.

'Let me see the map,' she said.

This time, Nat didn't refuse her. She studied it closely, seeing that the path of the cross-island route matched a narrow highway snaking between high peaks and all the way across the centre of the island.

'Look,' she said, nodding at the d-meter. It showed a d-field rating of zero. Yet they were already deeper into the island than Dutch would have believed possible until the last few days.

They drove on until the ocean disappeared from view and tall mountains arose around them. They climbed a mountain road dense with overhanging foliage, slowing from time to time to skirt around boulders that had come tumbling down from on high over the years. It made for slow going, and Dutch felt sure they'd be toast if they encountered any more kaiju, but even so they got past the worst of it. There seemed little doubt that within a few years, erosion and rockfall would make the inland roads forever impassable.

Then, at last, they came to a road high above a valley and saw an ethereal glow coming from behind a mountain peak a little further ahead. They got out of the Coupé, walking to the edge of the road and looking towards it.

'Is that it?' asked Dutch. 'The Rift?'

'Can't be anything else.'

She shook her head. 'In all the years I've been coming here, this is the first time I ever saw it with my own two eyes.' It looked like a column of fire, reaching up to the clouds. It shifted and changed, the contrast of shadows and colours somehow suggestive, as if on the cusp of resolving into objects or some kind of landscape.

Dutch's voice was halting when she spoke. 'What Elektron said about the Rift –'

'Elektron was crazy.'

'Still, you must have sometimes wondered yourself what it is.'

He shook his head. 'No.'

She looked at him in surprise. 'You can't be serious. Not even once?'

Even as she asked the question, she could see he was telling the truth.

She had a sudden memory, of being in her Dad's garage and hearing the first reports coming in over the radio that a nuke had hit Teijouan. No one had ever figured out what really happened, not with the d-field to keep those willing or brave enough to find out far from the island's centre.

But if Strugatsky's expedition had made it all the way to the Rift… Who could say what they'd found there?

They continued on to the village Nat had mentioned. By then night had fallen, and Dutch almost drove straight through it before she realised the few scattered shells of buildings strung along the roadside in fact constituted a settlement.

She pulled over, but kept the engine turning over. Her vision remained clear, with no shapes crowding the edges of her vision. The knowledge she had come so far, so much farther than anyone else had ever managed since the days of the evacuation, made her euphoric.

Beside her, Nat studied a notebook he'd pulled out of his driving suit by the light of a torch. Dutch glanced at the notebook and observed tight lines of spidery handwriting.

He looked up. 'There should be a general store straight ahead of here.'

Dutch took the brake off and coaxed the Coupé a little further along the narrow, bumpy road. Seeing more than a few metres without headlights was near to impossible, but no way was she risking turning them on.

'Here,' said Nat, his voice taut.

They pulled over and got out. The store appeared to be little more than a tin shack, its shelves still piled high with ageing canned goods.

Nat studied the notebook again.

'What is that?' Dutch asked.

'This? It belonged to that scientist they recovered.' He switched the torch off. 'The RV should be around the next corner.'

Dutch followed him around past the store to a row of small, pitiful-looking houses that weren't much more than shacks themselves. Thin saplings pushed through the windows, their roofs green with moss. He led her further, down a narrow, muddy lane that led to an empty lot occupied by a couple of rusted cars and an articulated RV of much more recent design.

A ladder beneath a door set into the side of the RV led up and inside its darkened interior. Dutch stood back as Nat ascended the steps, flicked on his torch, and looked around.

He reappeared within moments, one hand clamped over his face. He made his way over to the edge of the lot and retched into the grass.

'What did you see?'

He wiped his mouth and coughed. 'There's a body. The smell's pretty bad.'

She stepped towards him. 'Give me your torch.'

He passed it over and Dutch pulled a bandana out of her jeans, wrapping it tight over her mouth and nose before taking her turn to look inside the truck. She saw workbenches and scientific equipment, and a body sprawled on the floor. If she kept her breathing even and shallow and didn't breathe through her nose, she could just about bear the stink of putrefaction. Even so, she pulled off her bandana and sucked down a deep lungful of jasmine-scented air the moment she stepped out into open air.

'That's one dead in the truck and another dead not long after he got rescued,' she said. 'How many others were in the expedition?'

'Four.'

So there'd been six to start with. 'Elektron seemed to think they'd all somehow passed through the Rift.'

Nat groaned. 'I don't know why you even let him talk.'

She heard a rustling in the trees and glanced up. A pair of tiny eyes looked down at her and blinked, and then their owner shot off along a branch. Nothing more than a squirrel, but any normal animal was a rarity on Teijouan these days. That, even more than the car's d-meter, convinced her they were safe.

What was it Elektron had told her? That the Rift was a crossroads, with a million different roads. She remembered talking to some scientist at a pre-race event in Hong Kong, years before. He'd told her there were multiple worlds, each one a little bit different from the last. All stacked up one on top of another in some complicated way she couldn't make sense of. And Elektron himself had been a scientist long before his mind fractured.

Maybe there was even a world out there where her father hadn't died too young of a premature heart attack. A world where she hadn't had to fight her way through a succession of orphanages.

She went to sit on the hood of a derelict car and wished she had a cigarette, even though she'd given up years before.

'I need to keep looking and see what I can find,' said Nat, nodding at the bandana she held in one hand. 'Mind if I borrow that?'

She listened to him clatter around inside the truck for a while, then wandered back over to the grocery store, searching around until she found several cartons of cigarettes tucked away in a dry place. She pulled a carton open and lit a cigarette from a plastic lighter she found in a drawer, then got back inside the Coupé, steering it next to the RV. Nat ducked his head out and gave her an appreciative nod, then tossed down a fat refuse bag that landed next to one wheel. Dutch got out and took a look inside: he'd stuffed it full of hundreds more of the superconductor rods.

'Looks like you got what you were looking for,' she said, perching on the hood of the Coupé while she finished her cigarette.

'I guess.' He went back in, mouth and nose still covered by Dutch's bandana, and re-emerged with an armful of document folders. He dumped them on the hood next to Dutch. One fell open, pages of printed equations and dense handwriting flapping in a breeze.

'So what now?' she asked, sliding back off the hood.

Nat sorted through the folders and spread one open on the hood. 'There's another map here, showing the exact route to where they found these rods.'

'You want to steal more?'

His face stiffened at the comment. 'As many as the Coupé can carry.' He tapped the page with a fingernail. 'But it's right up next to the Rift – we'd be closer to it than anyone ever thought possible.'

Dutch couldn't make up her mind whether the idea excited

or terrified her. Maybe both, she decided. 'How far?'

'Five, six kilometres.'

'Sure thing,' she said, taking a last, shaky draw on her cigarette.

He nodded. 'We'll find a place for the night and set out at dawn.'

Dutch ground the cigarette under one boot. 'I wonder where the others are by now.'

'Who? The other contestants?'

'Nothing wrong with wondering.' They'd be holing up for the night round about now. As soon as the sun rose they'd take the road south. The terrain from that point on was smooth and level all the way to the finishing line. Sometimes the last leg turned into a straight contest of speed, with few if any kaiju encounters.

'Forget about the race,' he growled.

'We still need to cross the finishing line eventually,' she reminded him.

'We'll come in last,' he said, loading the folders into the boot.

*I've never come last*, thought Dutch. But then again, she'd never come first either. 'Why even bother with the subterfuge any more?' she asked. 'It's not like Strugatsky doesn't know you stole his map. He'll know we took the shortcut –'

'We *stick to the plan*, Dutch.'

'Sure,' she said, not looking at him. She nodded across the road. 'There's another hotel over there looks like it's still intact. We can hole up there.'

'I'm serious,' he said, gazing at her with a fixed expression. 'This is *not* about winning a race.'

'I know,' she said irritably. 'I won't bring it up again.'

He stood there unmoving for several more moments, eyes still fixed on her, then popped the hood and pulled a solenoid loose before holding it up where she could see it.

Her mouth fell open, and she laughed. 'You can't be serious.'

'I know you don't trust me,' he said, grinding the words out, 'and I understand why. But that doesn't mean I have to trust you either.' He pushed the solenoid into a pocket. 'This keeps us on the same page.'

Broken glass covered the floor of the hotel lobby, the walls decorated with posters of waving palm trees and advertisements for a local waterfall that had once been a tourist attraction. A corpse lay curled up behind the reception desk, its bones gleaming in what little moonlight found its way inside.

A number of the rooms, upon investigation, proved to be in decent enough condition, and in a few cases still retained their window-glass. Dutch found one with a double-bed that she could almost imagine had been made up in the last few hours. She tested it with her bodyweight. It creaked a little, but at least it didn't collapse into dust and splinters.

She sprawled back and listened to Nat moving around in the room next door, then lit another cigarette before heading back down. She'd seen a sign for a bar tucked out of sight behind the reception. To her delight, she discovered an unopened bottle of whisky.

She nodded to the corpse behind the reception desk on her way back upstairs and told it to put the whisky on the tab.

Back in her room she kicked off her boots and drank the whisky until a warm glow worked its way inside her. Nat had fallen silent next door. She thought about her long years in prison, and then she thought some more, and then she capped the whisky before heading through to Nat's room.

Nat lay sprawled and snoring on the bed in the next room. The window-glass had survived intact, but had been badly starred. He'd pulled ragged, half-rotted curtains closed and stripped down to a T-shirt and boxers.

He'd discarded his jacket over the back of a chair. Dutch made a fast search through his pockets but to her frustration couldn't find the solenoid. She stared at Nat's supine form for a moment longer, then turned towards the door.

A floorboard creaked. She looked back at Nat to see his eyes were open.

He sat up, blinking and regarding her with wary caution. 'Dutch? What is it?'

*Hi, Nat*, she imagined herself saying. *I was just searching through your stuff because I trust you even less than you think I do. In fact, I'm pretty sure you're going to try and kill me, and I'd rather get the hell out of here before you get the chance.*

'You looking for the solenoid?' he asked.

'No,' she lied.

'Then what?'

Dutch thought hard for a moment, then stepped closer, pulling her T-shirt up and over her head before dropping it on the chair where Nat's jacket hung. Her jeans followed, and then she climbed onto the bed, straddling him.

'This means nothing,' she said, looking down at him.

He looked up at her in silence, then brought his hands up to rest on her hips before giving her a single small nod.

'Just so we've got that clear,' she said, reaching for the clasp of her bra.

# ENDLESS HIGHWAY

Dutch woke shortly after dawn to the sound of someone screaming.

She stumbled upright and pressed her face against the starred glass in Nat's room. The dawn sky looked like a painted backdrop, the streets below a hastily constructed set. Nat stood in the road in front of the hotel, looking past the scientist's RV.

She heard the same voice cry out again, full of anguish and terror, from somewhere on the other side of the RV. Nat ran past the vehicle and out of sight.

Dutch got dressed fast and threw herself down the steps and outside. She came to a halt in the middle of the street and looked around, hearing nothing but the wind.

'Nat!'

No response.

*Leave him here*, she told herself. He'd left the map in the car. She could take it and drive away without him. Wu would have to believe her when she said he died in the jaws of a kaiju.

But then, she thought, grinding her teeth together until they hurt, he still had the solenoid. Without that, the Coupé wasn't going anywhere.

She ran over to the Coupé and grabbed a .375 hunting rifle out of the back. She tried hard to ignore the rush of fear down her spine like a flood of frozen diamonds as she loaded the rifle.

She found a narrow alley past the lot, with high walls on either side. At its far end, at the foot of a path that wound deeper into the forest slopes, crouched none other than Jack Burton. He had one hand pressed tightly over an open wound in his chest, his eyes pleading when he looked at her.

Dutch lifted the rifle and shot him straight between the eyes. She'd tried to brace herself, but the recoil still sent her stumbling backwards. A .375 was enough to take out an elephant.

She landed on her rump. Burton had vanished, replaced by another shapeshifter-kaiju. Blood streamed from a wound where one of its eyes had been. It started to crawl towards her, the smell of its breath like a charnel house in hell.

Nat jumped down from the right-hand wall and ran towards her. He got her back upright, and then they both ran around the corner to the Coupé. Dutch pushed the hood open, and Nat hurriedly replaced the solenoid before joining her inside the car.

Dutch had barely got the engine running when Anna Dubachev came stumbling around the corner towards the rear of the Coupé, hands reaching towards them as if in supplication.

Dutch laughed out loud and reversed the Coupé straight into her. The mirage faded, and the injured kaiju screamed its rage as they drove away at speed.

She still hadn't stopped laughing by the time they left the village behind them. Nat glared at her, his face streaked with sweat and blood.

'I hope to Christ it's not me you're laughing at,' he said.

'It would take forever to explain,' she gasped. 'Now tell me what the hell you think you were doing, taking a stupid chance like that.'

His face reddened. 'It made me think one of the other scientists had survived.'

She chuckled. 'Idiot.'

He looked out the window. 'You don't need to tell me.'

They headed towards the column of light over the next hill, and Dutch decided she had to kill Nat before he had a chance to kill her.

But first, she needed the answers to some questions.

By now, they were almost at the island's centre, and halfway to the East Coast. The light from the Rift grew stronger as they steered through jungle-strewn roads. The road ascended a mountainous slope through a series of steep switchbacks, and Dutch pulled over at the sight of a metal handcart abandoned on the road dead ahead. A body lay next to it, wearing a torn jumpsuit much like the one in the RV had been wearing.

Nat got out and looked around. Dozens of grey rods lay scattered all around the handcart, and thousands more on the surrounding slopes. Dutch caught sight of a shattered wreck half-buried in the trees that looked like a flying saucer, but of course couldn't possibly be.

She left Nat to gather up more of the rods and walked a little further up the road. This close, the Rift was so bright it hurt to look at it. She kept walking until she could look down into a shallow bowl of land where the road dipped back down.

The Rift took the form of a column of blazing, shifting light that rose from the floor of the valley, as if someone had captured the Northern Lights and put them on display where few might ever find them. What looked to be the ruins of a hospital sat in the valley's centre, barely visible amidst the penetrating brilliance.

*A secret facility*, Elektron had said. She was starting to think he hadn't been lying at all. She discerned shapes in the shifting patterns of light and shadow that seemed to be on the verge of resolving into… something.

The light shimmered, coalesced, and then did in fact become something.

She heard Nat walk up beside her, and she reached inside her jacket, feeling the contours of the pistol she'd put there before getting out of the car. 'What do you see?' she asked, nodding at the light.

He made a dismissive sound. 'I don't know. Coloured lights or something.'

She turned to stare at him. 'You must see *something*?'

He gave her a strange look. 'Now you're talking like Elektron. Maybe the d-field *is* frying your brain.'

He didn't ask what she saw, but if he had, she'd have told him she saw a road, long and straight and reaching towards a distant horizon, superimposed over the valley like a double exposure. The more she looked, the more solid the road became, and the less real the valley.

Somehow, Dutch knew in the centre of her soul that the road had an objective existence, and that somewhere beyond that long stretch of virgin tarmac a whole new world lay waiting for her, the same way it had been waiting for the scientists who disappeared – and the same way it would have been waiting for Elektron, if he'd managed to get this far.

If Elektron knew about this, then surely others would before long. What would happen once word got out about the Rift's true nature? Maybe it had always been waiting for people like her, the misfits and freaks who came to Teijouan for the Devil's Run because there were so few places left in the world where they could fit in. Most of them had been reduced to picked-clean piles of bones along Teijouan's deserted highways, but more would come – many more.

She noticed a set of stone steps cut into the hillside below the road, leading down to the hospital complex. She moved towards them.

Nat grabbed her by the arm and pulled her back. 'Where the hell do you think you're going?'

She laughed. 'Are you serious? Is a bunch of weird fireworks really all you see?'

'It's the d-field,' he said. 'It's making you see things that aren't there. You still need to get me back to the finishing line.'

'I wasn't going anywhere.'

'Like hell you weren't. I've seen you drive enough to know I've got a far better chance of making it back home with you behind the wheel.'

He was only partly wrong, she realised: she *had* been ready to go down there and find out where the road she'd seen in her vision led to. But there were still things she had to do first.

She turned to face him. 'So are we really just going to sit around and wait long enough for the others to drive over the finishing line before we cross it?'

'Yes.'

She laughed. 'Like fuck we are.'

His hands formed into fists. 'Dutch, I'm warning you. Do what I tell you, or I'll…'

'You'll what?' She locked her gaze with his. 'Kill me?'

She saw the tiniest glint of surprise as if she'd caught him red-handed. It wasn't much, but for Dutch, it was enough. She took out the pistol she'd secreted within her jacket before getting out of the car and shot him at point-blank range.

Nat stumbled backwards, then fell onto his back, one hand clutching at his shoulder. Blood seeped out across his shirt under the jacket.

'What the fuck?' he shouted, staring up at her. 'You *shot* me?'

She kept the gun trained on him. 'I'm pretty sure it's not a fatal wound. Not yet, anyway. Now tell me how long you've been working for Muto.'

His expression became incredulous. 'What?'

'I want to hear you say it.' She fought to keep her aim steady. 'I didn't forget how you insisted we check the car a second time right after we landed on Teijouan. I figure you put a nick in that hose in case I got suspicious of you. You wanted me to think someone else was gunning for me.'

Nat licked his lips. 'Listen, Dutch. This is the d-field, not you. We'll get to the end of the race, and we'll talk all this out over some beers. Okay? There's no need to point that thing at me.'

'I'll make a deal,' she said. 'If you tell me right now you're carrying one of Muto's death notices, I'll let you live; as long as you show it to me. I'll even let you ride back with me, although you'll be bound and gagged the whole damn way. But lie to me…'

He didn't answer, and she stepped towards him, pushing the pistol's barrel against his temple.

'Okay, okay!' He shouted. 'In one of my boots. The left one.'

*Of course.* She waited while he unlaced his boot and pulled it off. He threw the folded-up red envelope on the road in front of her.

'I want to know how you wound up working for Muto.'

He sighed. 'It's not that simple. Once he knew Wu had stolen the maps from him, Strugatsky came to me and made it clear I had to bring the rods to him instead of Wu. The alternative was an unmarked grave.'

Dutch felt she should have been surprised by that, but she wasn't. 'And killing me on Muto's behalf was, what…? A sideline?'

'Not exactly.' Nat's skin had grown paler, his eyes unfocused. Shock from the bullet-wound, she figured. 'I didn't even know there was any kind of animosity between you and Muto until that ninja asshole tried to kill you.'

'You recognised Muto's name when I mentioned it back in Japan,' she said. 'Few would have. So how did you know about her?'

'All I knew was Strugatsky hired Muto to find out who stole his maps, just like Elektron said. After you killed the ninja and you mentioned Muto, I went to see her –'

'When?' Dutch interrupted.

'Right after you stole the car and drove us back to the hotel. I told her I was working for Strugatsky too. I said she had to call off the dogs.'

Dutch thought. 'Because you needed me alive to get you to the Rift?'

'Yes. Can I please have the first-aid kit?'

'No. You still haven't told me how you wound up working for Muto as well as Strugatsky.'

'I didn't exactly have a choice, Dutch. She made it very clear if I didn't kill you and bring back proof, I'd be the one receiving death notices.'

For a moment – a very brief one – Dutch felt a stab of sympathy for the man bleeding out before her. 'And how does Elektron fit into all this?'

'He doesn't. Him working for Muto took me by surprise just as much as you. I don't think Muto's big on sharing information with her employees.'

'I'll tell you why,' Dutch snarled. 'She figured if Elektron botched the job, you'd be on standby to complete it. The only thing I can't figure out is how you were going to double-cross Wu if Harry had been my navigator.'

'I knew I'd have to find a way to make sure I took Harry's place,' said Nat. 'You fixed that for me real good, Dutch. So are you going to let me back up or not?'

She fought back a rush of sour phlegm. 'Damn you to hell.' *How long did you mean to wait before you killed me?* She wondered. *Until the last minute, when we were almost in sight of the Security Zone? Or before that?*

Dutch pictured Nat standing over her and taking a picture of her corpse with the Polaroid as evidence for Muto that she was dead, and felt her finger tighten on the trigger.

Then she saw Nat's eyes grow wide, as if he'd caught sight of something behind her. A shadow fell across them, and Dutch turned to see a monstrous shape arise from out of the Rift. The highway she'd glimpsed was gone, replaced by a hellish vision of unfamiliar stars above a barren and lifeless landscape.

The sun raced across the sky, day to night and back again in seconds, and by the time the sky had stopped strobing the kaiju had crossed over. It reared up to its full height, the ground shaking as it took its first, tentative step into its new home.

She remembered about Nat too late. He threw himself on her, one arm tight under her chin and his free hand reaching for her eyes. She tried to twist away, panicking because she knew he meant to blind her.

The kaiju let out a roar like a thousand years of thunder and death all compressed into one terrible moment. Rocks and gravel came tumbling down the slope of the hill above the road, almost hitting them and spraying them with gravel.

Dutch took the chance to twist free. Nat ran towards the Coupé, stumbling from side to side as he did so and leaving a crimson trail.

The kaiju took another lumbering step towards them. Dutch chased after Nat, knowing she had at best moments before the beast killed them both.

She beat him to the Coupé, but he yanked the door open before she could reach for the ignition. She punched him hard, then slammed the door against him, sending him reeling like a drunkard. He took a faltering step backwards and collapsed.

Dutch pumped the gas firmly with one foot until the ignition caught. She could see the kaiju reaching down towards her, flame flickering deep within its gaping jaws…

The tyres span and caught the tarmac. She drove past the kaiju, the night turning bright as flames came bursting from between its jaws. She urged the Coupé to go faster, leaning over the wheel like a jockey urging a horse towards its final hurdle.

From far behind, she thought she heard the sound of screaming.

The beast faded into the distance, but she didn't slow down, taking hairpin turns at speeds that would have terrified her if she'd let herself think about it. She kept going until the first glimmer of the sea appeared off to the East, then pulled over onto the side of the road to lean her head against the wheel, deep sobs racking her until she felt drained of all fear. Then she reached over to the glove compartment and pulled out the navigator's maps.

From there the road wound down towards the coast like a black tar snake, looping over hills and around small mountains until the terrain became more level. The d-field began to assert itself again, but not so much she couldn't still navigate.

At one point she saw Nat standing beneath the shade of a banyan tree, lurching towards her with pain in his eyes and blood pouring from his shoulder wound. She floored the gas and caught a glimpse of the shapeshifter's outline flowing and changing in the rearview mirror. Then she came to the coast and parked in the shade of some trees, watching from a safe distance as a Spine-back lumbered through lush jungle, trees shaking and splintering as it brushed past them.

To her astonishment, she was the first to arrive at the second rendezvous. The supply crates were still tangled up in parachutes that billowed across a yellow sandy beach.

Right then, Dutch realised she could win the race. She stared out to sea for a minute, watching the waves roll up to the shore and letting the thought wash through her. Then she hunted around until she found a crowbar duct-taped to a crate, and before long spare fuel, more bottles of water and a box of protein bars were all hers.

The hours that followed passed in a blur. Dutch kept the gas pedal low to the floor. A storm had raged across the eastern coast of Teijouan, sweeping smaller debris off the highways and leaving them clearer than usual. The terrain on the East Coast was less mountainous, and hence much easier to negotiate.

A Venomosaurus chased her for a while a hundred kilometres from the finishing line, and the Coupé lost a fender before she found a place to hide out deep in a maze of alleys. That cost her most of an hour, but she could feel in her bones that she remained in the lead.

Then, at long last, she saw the steel fence of the Security Zone up ahead, sunlight glinting from the lenses of news cameras peeking over the top. Deep gouges in the soil suggested some shelling had been necessary in order to dissuade some inquisitive kaiju from approaching any closer. The gate rolled up at her approach, and she crossed into the Security Zone, trailed by a fanfare of recorded trumpets and cheers.

She got out, tired and bloody and dusty, and raised both arms in triumph before turning to pat the Coupé's hood, like an old and faithful dog. Technicians came running up, yanking open the boot and lifting out the canisters of film stored there. They also pulled the film from the Coupé's rear and front-mounted cameras, hurrying down to the shore to where idling motorboats waited.

*I'm not quite finished with you*, she thought, her fingers stroking the Coupé's steel flanks.

'And it's a *fantastic* end to this year's Devil Run!' Wayne Wilson bellowed into his microphone. 'Coming first for the first time in her life, days after being released from prison, it's Dutch McGuire in a sensational, record-breaking win! After she disappeared past Shinchiku, we all figured Dutch had gone to the great racecourse in the sky, right up until her miraculous reappearance several hundred kilometres further along the race route. I don't know if *anyone's* ever going to be able to beat a time like that!'

Dutch blinked as a galaxy of lights snapped and popped all around. Wilson appeared before her, his bleached hair arranged in a coif that balanced atop his head as if in defiance of gravity, a microphone gripped in one fist.

'Dutch,' he said, grabbing her hand and pumping it up and down, 'congratulations! You've broken every record going, and you're at least thirteen hours ahead of the other competitors – the fastest time ever recorded in the Devil's Run and one most people might even call *impossible*. You disappeared from the race for the longest time – what happened?'

He pushed the microphone toward her. She blinked at it, feeling dazed. 'I found a shortcut.'

'A –' For a moment, Wilson appeared almost lost for words. 'A *shortcut*? Am I hearing you right, Dutch – that there's a way *across* the island, despite the Rift and the d-field?'

'Yeah.' She found it hard to think, with all the reporters shouting questions at her.

Then she remembered something.

'One second,' she said, leaning back into the car and snatching up the map. Then she opened the boot and lifted out the sack of grey superconductor rods, hoisting it over her shoulder. Then she looked around until she could see Adam Lin and his fellow protestors and made her way over to them.

Wilson followed in her wake, trailed by cameramen. 'How did you find this shortcut, Dutch?' Wilson yelled into his microphone. 'Isn't this incredible, ladies and gentlemen? I never in a million years thought I'd see a day like this. Did you see the Rift? How did you survive the d-field? What did it – hey, Dutch!'

Lin stood behind a wooden barrier manned by several soldiers keeping him and the protestors at bay. He watched in amazement as Dutch skirted around the barrier before dropping the sack at his feet.

Lin stared at the sack, then at Dutch, a megaphone clutched in his hand. 'What is this?'

'Something that Strugatsky and Wu want very much,' she said. 'I'd look after it if I were you. I figure it's worth a couple of billion dollars.'

Lin leaned down and opened the sack looking inside. 'I don't understand. What is this?'

'All I know is, Wu and Strugatsky think it's worth killing for. Here.' She pushed the map into his hands. 'This tells you where to find more. It's a safe route across the island.'

Lin's expression shifted from confusion to something more subtle and cunning. 'Why are you doing this, Miss McGuire?'

'Someone's got to look out for Teijouan, right?'

Then she turned on her heel without another word and walked back the way she'd come.

The reporters were still shouting questions at her, and cameras still snapped and clicked, but they were getting less vocal as they realised they weren't going to get anything out of her. Wilson watched, perplexed, as she slid behind the wheel of the Coupé.

'Where are you going, Dutch?' Wilson demanded, pushing his microphone in the open window of her car. 'The race is over!'

She reached out and snatched the microphone from his hand. 'Listen up, assholes,' she shouted, her own voice reverberating back at her. 'Some things are too important to leave in the hands of people whose sole defining quality is the size of their bank account. Like, I don't know, the fate of the world, maybe, or something that could revolutionise science or, or… whatever. Anyway, I figure that kind of shit belongs to all of us.'

She dropped the microphone into the dirt at Wilson's feet and it sent up a yowl of feedback. She reached out and adjusted her mirror until she could see Lin and his fellow protestors running down the beach to a waiting Zodiac, hauling the sack between them.

The engine caught on the first try, and she reached for the clutch. 'Hey!' yelled Wilson, snatching the microphone back up. 'Where the hell are you going, Dutch?'

She flashed him a brilliant smile. 'Home,' she said, then took off back the way she'd come in a cloud of exhaust smoke.

By luck, they hadn't got around to lowering the gate again.

A couple of hours later, heading north on the East Coast road, she passed the Countess, her car's chassis torn as if it had been raked by huge claws. Dutch had a brief glimpse of her gaping open-mouthed as she sped past in the opposite direction. Not long after, she found her way back inland, the d-meter a steady safe blue the whole way.

Sometime in the early evening she at last saw the flickering lights of the Rift. She drove down into the valley, and watched as the shimmering light shifted and changed, once again becoming a long stretch of highway beneath a calm and moonlit night. As if it had been waiting for her.

Maybe it had, she thought. One way or the other, she'd find out. She kept driving towards where she'd seen the ruins of the facility, but by the time she got there it had vanished. So had Teijouan: the Coupé sat on a desert road, a tall sandstone butte visible in the distance. Somewhere beyond the horizon the lights of a city radiated a faint glow.

There'd be others following behind her. Of that, Dutch felt sure. Maybe some few of them might find their way to this very same road, the one out of all those millions the Rift had brought her to. She checked the fuel gauge: she still had a little gas. Not much, but she had faith that somewhere up ahead she'd find an open garage with tools and gas and maybe even a beer.

She wound down the window and drove towards the dawn, letting the breeze catch her hair.

# ABOUT THE AUTHOR

Gary Gibson is the author of fourteen books, including *Stealing Light* (first in the four volume Shoal Sequence), *Extinction Game*, and the NewCon Press novella *Ghost Frequencies,* and various short stories. A native of Glasgow, he currently lives in Taipei. He has a blog and website at: www.garygibson.net.

# SELECTED BIBLIOGRAPHY:

Angel Stations (2004)
Against Gravity (2005)
Ghost Frequencies (2018)

<u>Shoal Sequence</u>
1 Stealing Light (2007)
2 Nova War (2009)
3 Empire of Light (2010)
4 Marauder (2013)

<u>The Final Days</u>
1 Final Days (2011)
2 The Thousand Emperors (2012)

<u>The Apocalypse Duology</u>
1 Extinction Game (2014)
2 Survival Game (2016)

# NEW FROM NEWCON PRESS

**Simon Morden – Bright Morning Star**

A ground-breaking take on first contact from scientist and novelist Simon Morden. Sent to Earth to explore, survey, collect samples and report back to its makers, an alien probe arrives in the middle of a warzone. Witnessing both the best and worst of humanity, the AI probe faces situations that go far beyond the parameters of its programming, and is forced to improvise, making decisions that may well reshape the future of a world.

**Kim Lakin-Smith – Rise**

Denounced by her own father and charged with crimes against the state, Kali Titian – pilot, soldier, and engineer – is sentenced to Erbärmlich prison camp, where she must survive among her fellow inmates the Vary, a race she has been raised to consider sub-human; a race facing genocide; a race who until recently she was routinely murdering to order. A potent tale of courage against the odds and the power of hope in the face of racial intolerance.

**Ian Whates – Dark Angels Rising**

The Dark Angels – a notorious band of brigands turned folk heroes who disbanded a decade ago – are all that stands between humanity and disaster. Reunited, Leesa, Jen and their fellow Angels must prevent a resurrected Elder – last of a long dead alien race – from reclaiming the scientific marvels of his people. Supported by a renegade military unit and the criminal zealots Saflik, the Elder is set on establishing itself as God over all humankind.

**RB Kelly – Edge of Heaven**

Creo Basse, a city built to house the world's dispossessed. In the dark, honeycomb districts of the lower city, Turrow searches for black-market meds for his epileptic sister when he encounters one of the many ways Creo can kill a person. A tinderbox of unrest finally ignites when a deadly plague breaks out, which the authorities claim is a terrorist weapon manufactured by extremist artificial humans hiding in the city, but is the truth darker still?